THE THREE-ARCHED BRIDGE

ISMAIL KADARE, born in 1936 in the Albanian mountain town of Gjirokastra near the Greek border, studied in Tirana and at the Gorky Institute, Moscow. He is Albania's best-known poet and novelist. His works have been translated world-wide. He established an uneasy *modus vivendi* with the Communist authorities until their attempts to turn his reputation to their advantage drove him in October 1990 to seek asylum in France, for, as he says, "Dictatorship and authentic literature are incompatible . . . The writer is the natural enemy of dictatorship." Ismail Kadare will have been a considerable influence in bringing about the fall of the Albanian Communist regime. *The Three-arched Bridge* was completed in Tirana in 1978.

JOHN HODGSON studied English at Cambridge and Newcastle and has taught at the universities of Prishtina and Tirana.

Ismail Kadare

THE
THREE-ARCHED
BRIDGE

*Translated from the Albanian
by John Hodgson*

THE HARVILL PRESS
LONDON

First published in Albanian with the title *Ura me tri harqe*
and in France in 1981 by Librairie Arthème Fayard

This edition, based on the revised 1993 text,
first published in Great Britain in 1998
2 Aztec Row, Berners Road
London N1 0PW

www.harvill-press.com

2 4 6 8 9 7 5 3 1

A CIP catalogue record for this book
is available from the British Library

ISBN 1 86046 463 7

Designed and typeset in Garamond at
Libanus Press, Marlborough, Wiltshire

Printed and bound in Great Britain by Butler & Tanner Ltd
at Selwood Printing, Burgess Hill

THE
THREE-ARCHED
BRIDGE

I

O tremble, bridge of stone
As I tremble in this wall.
—Ballad of immurement

I, THE monk Gjon, the sonne of Gjorg Ukcama, knowynge
that ther is no thynge wryttene in owre tonge about
the Brigge of the Ujana e Keqe, have decided, now that its
construction is finished and it has even been sprinkled twice
with blood, at pier and parapet, to write its story, the more
so as legends, falsehoods and rumours of every kind
continue to be woven around it.

Late last Sunday night, when I had gone out to walk on
the sandbank, I saw the idiot Gjelosh Uk-Markaj crossing
the bridge. He was laughing and sniggering to himself, and
gesticulating like mad. The shadow of his limbs pranced
over the roadway and flickered down the arches to the
water. I struggled to imagine what sort of impression all
these recent events might have left on his disordered mind,
and I told myself that people had no call to laugh whenever
they saw him muttering his way back and forth across the
bridge, clenching his fists and flicking his wrists with
the impression he was holding a horse's reins. The fact is,
what people know about this bridge is no less muddled than
the inventions of a madman's mind.

3

To stop people spreading truths and untruths about this bridge in the eleven languages of the peninsula, I will attempt to present the whole truth about it: in other words to record the lie we saw and the truth we did not see and to set down not only the daily events that are as ordinary as the stones from which it is built, but also the major disasters, which are about as many in number as the arches of the bridge.

Muleteers and caravans are now spreading all over the great land of the Balkans the legend of the sacrifice allegedly performed at the piers of the bridge. Few people know that this was not a sacrifice dedicated to the naiads of the waters, but just but a straighforward crime, to which, along with other things, I will bear witness before our millennium. I say millennium, because this is one of those legends that survives for more than a thousand years. It begins in death, and ends in death, and we know that news of death or rumour leavened by the yeast of death is of all things the least likely to fear death itself.

I write this chronicle in haste, because times are troubled, and the future looks blacker than ever before. After the chilling events at the bridge, people have calmed down a little and so have the times, but another evil has appeared on the horizon – the Turkish state. The shadows of its minarets are slowly stealing towards us.

This is an ominous peace, worse than any war. For centuries we had bordered on the ancient land of the Greeks; then suddenly, before we realized it and as if in a bad dream, we awoke one morning to find ourselves neighbours of the Empire of the Ottomans.

Its minarets shoot up on all sides, a veritable dark forest of them. I have a premonition that the destiny of Arberia

4

will soon change, especially after what happened this winter, when blood was shed for the second time on the newly-finished bridge – this time Asiatic blood. But everything will find its place in my chronicle.

2

AT THE beginning of March in the year 1377, on the right bank of the Ujana e Keqe, no more than fifty paces from the half-embedded stakes to whose iron cleats the ferry was moored every night, a traveller whom nobody in this district knew suffered an epileptic fit. The ferryman, an eyewitness to the scene, said that this scarecrow of a man – he looked like a saint or a madman – wandered a while along the riverbank between the jetty and the spot where the river is fordable in summer, then let out a sudden shriek as if his throat had been cut and fell backwards in the mud.

Even though this was the spot on the bank where people and livestock were used to embarking or disembarking from the ferry, it was still a mere backwater, a place where nothing out of the ordinary ever happened. Of course such things did happen, as they do at all crossing points, and never more so than at a place like this, where the ancient highway, which was of such great length that nobody knew where it came from, was suddenly cut off by the river. At all events, here important events were the exception. As a rule, people who gathered to cross the river simply waited here, as people do at such times. In bad weather they would mutely watch the swirling, dun-coloured waters of the river as they waited wrapped in sodden black skins. Even the harness bells of the horses alongside them gave out a feeble tinkle, and the children's voices were hushed as the raft approached. The appearance of the raft, with the ferryman squatting on board, served to frighten them.

A kind of wilderness stretched all around; the low riverbank, sandy and muddy by turns, receded into the distance dotted here and there with reed patches. There was not the smallest house round about; even the walls of our parish house were out of sight, while the nearest inn was a good mile off.

By the stakes where the raft was moored at night there was a metal plaque on which the words "Ferries and Rafts" were inscribed in crooked lettering. For many years since, such plaques had been put up everywhere, not only in the lands of our own liege lord, Count Stres of the Gjikas, or Stres Gjikondi, as they call him for short, but also far away, even beyond the state borders of Arberia, in other parts of the peninsula. This started in the winter of the year 1367, ten years before, when all the rafts used as ferries across rivers, estuaries, and lakes were bought up by a bizarre person who came from God knows where, and whose name nobody knows. They even say that he has no name apart from "Ferries and Rafts", which has sprouted up everywhere like a plant that takes root wherever there is water and moisture. They say that he has the same plaque with the same words even at his great house from which he manages his business, and that he even signs the notices and receipts with the same words "Ferries and Rafts", much as if they were his emblem, just as a white lion with a flaming torch between its teeth is the emblem of our own liege lord.

Once this new master bought up all the ferries and rafts the ferrymen and boatmen became his employees, apart from the odd exception, such as the wretched ferryman at the Stream of the Tree-Stumps, who would have starved sooner than accept a wage from this damned Jew. Just after the winter of 1367, this metal plaque appeared on our riverbank too, with the tolls for crossing inscribed on it: "Persons, one-half grosh. Horses, one grosh."

In times of drought, when the Ujana e Keqe subsided and turned to a trickle, travellers would use the ford to cross the river on foot, even when laden with sacks, to avoid paying the toll. But they were not uncommonly drowned, deceived by the river, which was not for nothing called Ujana e Keqe, "Wicked Waters". Weather-blackened memorial crosses were still to be seen on both sides of the river. They say that the owners of "Ferries and Rafts" were careful to plant such crosses on the bank for every person drowned, to remind other travellers of the price to pay if they tried to cross the river without their assistance.

Together with the raft, "Ferries and Rafts" had also bought the old jetty, a relic of Roman times. Blacksmiths had after a fashion repaired its iron cleats so that the ferryman could secure his craft the more easily, especially in winter.

The raft brought in large earnings, not only from the passage of travellers and their livestock, but also from the caravans that carried from Arberia to Macedonia the salt from the great coastal salt pans, and especially from the carts that supplied the Byzantine naval base at Orikum near Vlora. There had been detailed agreements dividing this income between our liege lord and "Ferries and Rafts". In fact there had never been the least hint of a quarrel over this point, a rare thing on the face of this earth. It seems that "Ferries and Rafts" was was ever scrupulous in business matters.

3

A SMALL crowd of people, both familiar faces and strangers, had gathered round the man who had fallen with the epileptic fit. He shook and frothed at the mouth as if straining to fling his limbs clean across the Ujana e Keqe, while flinging his head the opposite way. Someone made two or three attempts to hold down his head as they usually do in such cases, so that he would not crack his skull in his convulsions, but it was impossible to keep a purchase on that half-bald cranium.

"It is a sign from on high," said one of the bystanders. This was a thin man who, when we later asked what his business was, said he was a wandering fortune-teller.

"And what sort of sign is it?" someone else asked.

The man threw a lacklustre look at the trembling epileptic, then at the river.

"Yes," he muttered. "A sign from on high. Look how his trembling moves the waters, and the waters pass on their own movement to him. My God, they understand each other."

The bystanders looked at each other. The man on the ground seemed to be becoming calmer. Someone had a hold on his head now.

"Well, what sort of sign is it, what do you think?" someone else asked.

The man who said he was a wandering fortune-teller half closed his lifeless eyes.

"It is a sign from the Almighty that a bridge has to be built here, over these waters."

"A bridge?"

"Didn't you see how he stretched his arms in the direction of the river? And that his body shook, just as a bridge shakes when heavy carts pass over it?"

"Brr . . . It's cold," someone complained.

The sick man was quiet now, his limbs only occasionally twitching in their last spasms, as if they had wound down. Someone bent over and wiped the foam from the edges of his lips. His eyes were sad and dull.

"This is a holy sickness," the fortune-teller said. "In our parts, they call it the foaming. It always comes as a sign. The sign can portend evil and warn of an earthquake, for instance, but this time, praise God, the omen is a favourable one."

"A bridge . . . this is strange," people round about started saying. "Our liege lord must be told of this. Who is the lord of these parts? Count Stres of the Gjikas, long life to him. Are you a foreigner then, not knowing a thing like that? That's right, brother, from abroad. I was waiting for the raft when the poor fellow . . . This must certainly reach the ear of our liege-lord. A bridge? My goodness, who would have thought of it!"

4

THREE WEEKS later I was summoned urgently to the count. His great house, fortified at every corner with turrets, was only one hour's journey away. When I arrived, they told me to go straight up to the armorial hall, where our liege lord usually received princes and other nobles whose journeys brought them through his lands.

In the hall were the count, one of his scribes, our bishop, and two unknown house-guests dressed in tight-fitting jerkins, which were in fashion who knows where.

The count looked on edge. His eyes were bloodshot for lack of sleep, and I remembered that his only daughter had recently fallen ill. No doubt the two strangers were doctors from somewhere or other.

"I can't get through to them at all," he said as soon as I entered. "You know several languages. You can help us."

The new arrivals did indeed speak the most horrible tongue. My ears had never heard such a babble. Little by little I began to untangle the strands. I noticed that their numbers were Latin and their verbs generally Greek or Slav, while they used Albanian for the nouns, and now and then a word of German. Adjectives they altogether did without.

With difficulty I began to grasp what they were trying to say. They had both been sent by their master to our liege lord, the Count of the Gjikas, with a particular mission.

They had heard of the sign sent by the Almighty for the construction of a bridge over the Ujana e Keqe, and they undertook to build it, or in other words he, their master, was, if the count would give them permission. In short, they were prepared to build a stone bridge over the Ujana e Keqe within a period of two years, to buy the land on which it was to stand, and to pay the count a regular annual tax on the profits they would earn from it. If the count agreed, this would all be set out in a detailed agreement (item by item and point by point, as they put it) that would be signed and sealed by both parties.

They broke off their speech to produce their seal, which one of them drew from inside his strange jerkin.

"That which the Almighty proposes must be carried out," they said, almost in one voice.

The count turned his weary, bloodshot eyes first on the bishop and then on his own scribe. But this riddle left them looking impassive.

"And who is this master of yours?" our liege lord asked.

Out came a fresh tangle of words, but the threads were this time so snagged that it took me twice as long to comb them out. They explained that their master was neither a duke, a baron, nor a prince, but was a rich man who had recently bought the old bitumen mines abandoned since Roman times and had also bought the larger part of the equally ancient great highway, which he intended to resurface. He has no title, they said, but he has money.

They kept interrupting each other, and finally noted down on a piece of paper what sums they would pay for the land and what annual tax they would pay to exploit the bridge.

"But what matters of course is to heed the message of the Most High," one of them said.

The sums noted on the paper were fabulous, and everyone knew that our liege lord's revenue had recently declined. Moreover, his daughter had been ill for two months and the doctors could not diagnose her malady.

Our liege lord and the bishop repeatedly caught each other's eye. The count's thoughts were clearly fluctuating between his empty exchequer and his sick daughter, and the bridge these strangers were offering to build was the remedy for both evils.

They started talking again about the heavenly message conveyed by the vagrant. In our parts, they call the poor fellow's ailment moon-sickness, one of them explained, whereas here, as far as I can gather, it is called earth-sickness. Not that it makes much difference. These very names show clearly that everywhere they consider it a superior disorder, practically divine as one might say.

Our count did not think it over for long. He said that he accepted, and told his scribe to draw up the contract in Albanian and Latin. He then invited us all for luncheon, and I have never sat down to a grimmer one, as I kept having to rack my brains to grasp the ever more incomprehensible things these strangers were saying.

5

IN THE afternoon, I had the misfortune to accompany
them as far as the bank of the Ujana. I consoled myself
that at least I was no longer obliged to make sense of their
garbled pronouncements: Road no good, no maintain, all
mess. Water smooth itself, road non, routen need work,
we has no tales, has instruct, we fast money, give, take. Water
different, boat move itself graciosus, but vdrug many drown,
bye-bye, sto dhjavolos. Funebrum, he, he, road no, road sehr
guten but need gut repair.

Fortunately, now and then they shut their mouths. They
watched the flight of the storks. Then, seeing the granaries,
they asked about the size of the harvest and the number of
cattle taken to market and the route they took.

I noticed that the closer we came to the river, the less
talkative they became and the less spirited. As they waited
for the raft that was to carry them across, they did not
conceal their terror of the waters. This was evident at all
events from their faces.

Dusk was falling when they embarked on the ferry. I
stared after them from the bank for a while. They were
engaged in a frantic discussion, gesticulating like anything
and pointing at each bank of the river in turn. It was cold.
In the fast-falling darkness, they looked from a distance like
a few black lines scrawled on the raft, as mysterious and

incomprehensible as their inhuman gabble. And suddenly, as I watched them disappear, a suspicion crept into my mind, like a black beetle: the man who had fallen in a fit on the riverbank, the wandering fortune-teller who had been close by him, and these two clerks with their tight jerkins were in the service and pay of the same master . . .

6

As EXPECTED, the news of the bridge to be built over the Ujana e Keqe spread rapidly. Bridges had been built now and then in all sorts of places, but nobody remembered any of them causing so much commotion. They had been built with virtually not a word of comment, to the muffled sound of hammers on wood, that hardly differed from the monotonous croaking of the frogs round about Then, when they were finished, they served their purpose without exciting comment until they were carried away by a flood, struck by lightning or, still worse, until they decayed to the point that the traveller, having taken a first step on the rotten planks, would hesitate to take a second, but turn back in search of a raft or ford nearby to make his crossing. This was because all these had been wooden bridges, while the one now to be built was to be a real bridge in stone with several arches and a solid paved roadway, perhaps the first of its kind in the whole of Arberia.

People responded to the news with a feeling of fear mingled with elation. They were pleased that they would have no more dealings with those churlish ferrymen, who were always on the far bank when you wanted them, if they were to be found at all, and who, even worse, turned out to be drunk, with the exception of the present ferryman, the hunchback, who never pestered the women and never drank but always looked so forbidding he might have been ferrying you to your death. Besides, the rafts were filthy and damp and their rocking made you want to throw up, while the bridge would always be there, at all times of the day or night, ready to arch its stone back under your feet, without swaying or playing tricks. They would have no more trouble with the river either, which sometimes swelled and wreaked havoc, or else would dwindle to the merest thread, as if about to give up the ghost. People were glad that the Ujana e Keqe, which had been such a trial to them, would finally be pinned down in a stone collar. But this very thing, if it caused them joy, also scared them. It is not easy to saddle a kicking mule, let alone the Ujana e Keqe. Oh, we shall see, we shall see how it all turns out, they said.

And as always when events of this importance were in the offing, people began to pay each other more visits among their scattered houses; they even went further afield, to the Poplar Copse, where few had been since the Duke of Gjin had been ambushed there, shortly before the betrothal was broken off with the house of our liege-lord. There were others who went to the wild pomegranates, by the Five Wells, from where a roundabout route would bring them out at Mark Kasneci's clearing; here they would then roll up their breeches to cross the quagmire and come out on the highway. There, if the news really was such that they could not keep it to themselves, their legs simply carried them down the road to the Inn of the Two Roberts. There, everybody knew what happened: Gossip was rife.

There were some who were far from pleased about the bridge being built; they were quite distraught and came out with the most dire predictions, like Ajkuna, the old crone. "That bridge," she said, "is the devil's backbone – woe to any who dares set foot on it!"

7

A<small>T THE</small> end of March, one frosty morning (it was one of the last three saints' days of winter) I was once again summoned urgently to the count. I was terrified at the thought of those crazy jabberers coming back. I would have found it easier to interpret for woodpeckers. As I dozed in the cart I was ashamed to find myself idiotically mumbling the words of the old ballad, "Oh March wind, oh brother mine, blast these blathermouths on the washing line." Only, this time it was not them but the people from "Ferries and Rafts". There were three of them, one of whom, a lanky, pale man with a pointed beard, had little to say. Judging by the respect shown to him by the other two, he was one of the main directors of "Ferries and Rafts", and perhaps their great master's deputy. All three spoke perfect Latin. They carried black leather bags, full of all kinds of documents.

This time the count brought us into his study. Heavy oak bookshelves took up part of the walls, and I strained my eyes to read the titles of the books from a distance, in the hope of asking for one of them some time, should the chance arise.

"We fail to understand what complaint the noble count might have against us," said the Pointed Beard, not raising his eyes from his bag. "As far as I am aware, we have always fulfilled our agreement to the letter."

Two or three spots of colour appeared on the count's cheeks that had been bloodless since his daughter fell sick.

I had acted as interpreter for several conversations between the count and "Ferries and Rafts", and I knew well that it was always "Ferries and Rafts" that complained about our lord, and never the other way round. There had been continual complaints about the delayed repayment of sums borrowed by our liege lord from "Ferries and Rafts" since the time of the unfortunate campaign against the Duke of Tepelena. The bank of "Ferries and Rafts" had twice reduced the interest rate from fourteen to nine and then to six per cent, and had finally agreed to postpone the repayment of the loans for five years, without interest. They were forced into this against their will, because they did not want to create an open breach with the count, from which they would emerge the losers, since the count could make the quarrel a pretext for not paying back a single penny. Most princes did this now and then, and everybody knew that there was no power that could force the count to honour an agreement with a bank, even with one of the largest in Durrës, such as the bank of "Ferries and Rafts".

So when the bearded man mentioned the question of a complaint, our liege lord considered that the man was being ironic.

"What complaint?" he cried. "Who has been complaining about you?"

His tone implied, Have you grown so big-headed as to imagine I would stoop to making complaints against endless moaners like yourselves?

The man from "Ferries and Rafts" eyed him frostily.

"It is not a direct complaint, my noble count," he said.

"Then explain yourself," the count said.

The other gave him a fixed stare. His jaw appeared to be sheathed in his black beard, that seemed to keep his head straight.

"Sir, it is about a bridge," he said finally.

"Ah," the count said. The exclamation seemed to escape him involuntarily, and we all, who knows why, exchanged glances.

"A bridge, no less," the Pointed Beard repeated, as if doubting we had understood correctly. His piercing eyes never left the count.

"So that's what the matter is," the count said. "And what concern is it of yours?"

The "Ferries and Rafts" representative took a deep breath. It seemed that he needed something more than air to shape the required words of explanation. He began to speak slowly and, phrase by phrase, stated his opinion with increasing bluntness. In the end he put it baldly. "Ferries and Rafts" was against the construction of the bridge, because it severely damaged the company's interests. It was not just that the raft across the Ujana e Keqe would become redundant. No, something much more serious was at stake that harmed the entire system of ferries, or what the Latins called water transportation, that had made use of rafts and barges since time immemorial and was now concentrated in the hands of "Ferries and Rafts".

Our liege lord listened with an expression of indifference. The "Ferries and Rafts" spokesman weighed his words carefully. I found his pure Latin easy to translate, and even had plenty of time left over to think about what I heard. The visitor claimed that this stone bridge would be the first brutal injury (his exact words) ever inflicted on the free spirit of the waters. After that worse was (in his view) to be

21

expected. Nothing but disaster would come of putting the river in such horrible chains, as if it were a convict.

A more thoughtful look came into the count's eyes and he glanced at me for a moment. This seemed to register with the men from "Ferries and Rafts" ; for the rest of the discussion this was the aspect they harped on. They began to talk about bridges not only with aversion but as frankly dangerous objects.

Clearly the demon of the waters, in the person of "Ferries and Rafts", was in bitter enmity with the demon of the land, who built roads and bridges.

"Stop them trespassing in our domain," said Pointed Beard, "and we will be ready to renegotiate the outstanding loans."

Our liege lord studied his hands.

The words "stop them" were uttered with such ferocity by the man of the black beard, he might have been saying, "Kill them, slaughter them, hack them to pieces, let nobody dream of building a bridge on this land for the next forty generations!"

Some years previously, a monk from the Low Countries on his way home from Africa had told me about a deadly struggle between a crocodile and a tiger, which he had watched from the branches of a tree.

"We may even consider the possibility of deferring all your debts, over a very long period,"said Pointed Beard.

Our liege lord continued to stare down at the ring glittering on his finger.

"Or *sine die*," the other went on.

The Netherlander had told me how the two beasts, the tiger and the crocodile, had circled each other for a long time without being able to get in a bite or a blow at all.

"Besides, is the noble count aware of the nature of the business conducted by the man who wants to build this bridge?" asked Pointed Beard.

"That is of little interest to me," the count said with a shrug.

"Allow me to tell you nonetheless," Pointed Beard continued. "He is involved in the black arts."

Three times the tiger had thrown himself on the crocodile's back, and three times his claws slipped on the monster's hard scales. Yet the crocodile had been unable to bite the tiger or lash him with his tail. It seemed that the contest would never end.

"Of course," our liege lord said, "the bitumen he extracts is black."

"Black as death," Pointed Beard confirmed.

They must again have noticed that shadow of gloom in our liege lord's eyes, because they fell back again on evil premonitions. All three began to talk, interrupting each other to explain that one only had to look at those barrels loaded with that horrible stuff to know that only wizards could readily take to such a trade, and woe betide anyone who permitted carts to cross his land loaded with these barrels leaking drops of tar in the heat, splattering the roads, splattering? – nay, staining the roads with the devil's black blood. And these drops of pitch always sow disaster. Now it has become the raw material for war, and this great wizard is selling it everywhere, to the Turks and Byzantines on one hand, and to all the counts and dukes of Arberia on the other, fomenting quarrels on both sides.

"That's what that tar does, and you are prepared to let it pass right through your lands. It brings death. Mourning."

But in one of the crocodile's furious thrashes he exposed

his soft underbelly to the eyes of the tiger. With a terrifying roar he sprang once again on the crocodile and, taking advantage of another momentary exposure of the crocodile's belly, attacked with claws and teeth on the instant. Burying his head in his enemy's body and crazed by his blood, he tore through the bowels with amazing speed, until he reached the heart and tore it to pieces.

The three talked on, but I, who knew our liege lord, realized that he was no longer listening. Perhaps they had overplayed their hand and this lost the game. The count showed a moment's hesitation, but I knew he was not one readily to change his mind. The sum of money promised by the road company was greater than the entire profits to be derived from the water people. Besides, his daughter had shown signs of improvement since his decision to build the bridge.

"No," he said at last. "Enough said. The bridge shall be built."

They were struck dumb. Two or three times they waved their hands as though they were about to speak but they did nothing but close their bags.

The beast of the water was defeated.

8

A WEEK later, the master of roads and bridges bought the stretch of highway that belonged to our lord. Two other emissaries had been journeying without rest for three months and more through the domains of princes, counts, and pashas, buying up the great western highway that had once been called the Via Egnatia and was now called the Road of the Balkans, after the name the Turks have recently given to the entire peninsula, and which comes from the word "mountain". More than by the purpose of the Ottomans to assign a single name to all the countries and peoples of the peninsula, as if to devour them the more easily, I was amazed by our readiness to accept the new name. I always thought that this was a bad omen, and now I am convinced that it is worse than that.

Now down this road came its purchasers, their clothes and hair whitened by its dust. They had so far purchased more than half of it, piece by piece, and perhaps they would travel all summer to secure the rest. They paid for it in fourteen kinds of coinage, Venetian ducats, dinars, drachmas, lira, groschen, and so forth, making their calculations in eleven languages, not counting dialects. This was because the road passed through some forty principalities, great and small, and so far they had visited only twenty-six of them. More than buying it, they seemed to be winding it onto a reel, this ancient roadway so gouged and pitted by winters, summers, and neglect.

The highway was older than anyone could remember. In the past three hundred years or so, almost all the holy crusades had passed along it. They said that two of the leaders of the First Crusade, Robert Giscard, Count of Normandy, and Robert, Count of Flanders, had slept a night at the inn a mile down the road from us, which since then had been called "The Inn of the Two Roberts".

Tens of thousands of knights of the Second Crusade had also passed this way, and then the Third Crusade headed by Frederick Barbarossa, or Barbullushi as our yokels called him. Then came the interminable hordes of the Children's Crusade, the Fifth Crusade, the Seventh and Eighth, the Knights Templar, the Knights of St John the Hospitaller and of the Teutonic Order. Very old men remembered these last, not from the time when they were travelling to Jerusalem, for that was in the year 1190, but from about forty years ago, when they passed this way on their return to Europe.

A more motley crowd of men had never been seen, as old Ajkuna said. A slow, silent procession on their great horses, their breastplates patched with all kinds of scrap, which squeaked, krr, krr, as they rode, sometimes dripping rust in wet weather. They were returning northward to their own countries, with that creaking like a lament, leaving trickles of rust on the road like drops of discoloured blood. The old woman said that when they saw the first of their ranks, people began to call, "Ah, the 'Jermans' are coming, the 'Jermans' are coming." One hundred and fifty years had passed since they came this way on their journey to Jerusalem; but the stories about them that had passed by word of mouth were so accurate that people recognized the

"Jermans" as soon as they appeared again. Very old people said that this was what they were called when they first came – "Jermans", or people who talk as if in *jerm*, in delirium. Yet many people seem to have liked this name, because they say it is now used everywhere. According to our ancients, these people have even begun to call their own country "Jermani", which means the place where people gabble in delirium, or land of *jerm*. However, I do not believe that this name has such an origin.

All these things came to my mind piecemeal as the agreement was being concluded. They paid for every piece, yard by yard, in Venetian ducats, and in the end departed very pleased, as if they had acquired the road for nothing. And so, with muddied hair and filthy clothes, they went on their way.

The monk from the Low Countries had told me that the beast of the land, after gorging himself on the crocodile's heart, left the monster dead under its useless scales and, with bloodied muzzle, wandered off through the grassland as if drunk.

9

IMMEDIATELY after this, one overcast morning, two somewhat bewildered-looking travellers dismounted by the Ujana e Keqe from their heavily-laden mules. They asked some children playing nearby whether this river was indeed the Ujana e Keqe, unloaded their mules, and there and then began to dig holes in the ground, fixing long stakes in them. Towards noon, it was apparent that they were building a hut. They laboured all day, and nightfall found them still at work; but in the morning they were no longer there. There was only the lopsided hut, its door shut with a padlock.

This aroused general curiosity. Everybody, not just old people and children, clustered round it, peering through cracks and crevices in the planks to see inside. They turned away disappointed, shrugging their shoulders as if to say, "Strange, not a thing inside." Some people examined the padlock, fingered it, while others chided them, then shook their heads and left.

Four days passed in this way. Interest was waning fast, but on the fifth day it revived again even more strongly. In the morning, people discovered, or simply had a feeling, that the hut was no longer empty. There was no smoke or noise, but nonetheless it was felt that someone was inside. Somebody must have come during the night.

Nobody saw him all that day or the next. A damp mist swathed everything, and people who went to the hut and peered through chinks said that the stranger was huddled up inside, wrapped in fleeces.

He emerged only on the third day. He had a tousled, tightly curled mop of red hair, and pock-marked cheeks. He had the kind of eyes that somehow seem not to allow you to look straight into them. The sick glint that appeared in his eye as soon as it caught yours would leave you disconcerted. He walked along the riverbank for a long while, crossed to the other side on the raft, and walked there too, returning to shut himself in the hut again.

The following days people saw him wade into the river up to his knees, drive in small stakes of some kind, and lower some things like metal sheets into the water. He would study these carefully and then cup river mud in his hands again and again, letting it trickle through his fingers. Everyone realized that this could be none other than the architect, or as they said now, the engineer of the bridge.

He spent two weeks in the ramshackle hut, morose and uncommunicative.

People came from all sides to see him, and not only the curious or the idle, who can never have enough of novelties, but folk of all kinds: men came on their way to market, women cradling their newly born, cheesemakers who smelled of brine, and soldiers on the march. They stood on the banks near the black pebbles and the old jetty, and watched the man moving to and fro, wading into the water and climbing out again, then returning to the water with his strange tools, then back to the sandbank where he would bend down and furiously dash off figures and sketches.

Even though it was clear from a distance that he was

excitable (it sometimes seemed that he could hardly keep one hand from pestering the other), he paid not the slightest heed to the people who watched him for hours on end. He never once turned his head towards them. Even old Ajkuna, the only person who found the nerve to go up and threaten him, he treated with total unconcern. She tapped the ground in front of him two or three times with her stick to make him listen and, when he lifted his head from his scrawls, she cried: "What are you doing here? Are you not afraid of Him above?" And she raised her staff to heaven. Perhaps he did not understand a word she said, or perhaps did not care. Who's to say? What we do know is that he bent his head over his figures once more and did not raise it again.

When people realized that nothing ever distracted him, they talked out loud and expressed to his very face, right within earshot, their opinions about him and his work. "Ah, now he's passing the mud through his hands, and he wants to know what sort of soil this is," explained someone. "Because land is like a human being, it can be strong or weak, healthy or sick. It can look fine from the outside, but still be diseased inside. And the soil itself can't tell whether what it carries will be for good or ill, and so he's running it through his fingers, to learn its secrets."

On they talked while he continued as indifferent as before. The first person to break the ice was Gjelosh the idiot. Without anybody telling him, without anybody understanding how, without a word he made himself adjutant to the stranger. He would wait for him to leave his hut at dawn, and carry his stakes and other implements, taking them to the riverbank and back again to the hut. Gjelosh was under his feet all day, and this taciturn redhead, who seemed ready to gnaw off his own fingers whenever the work hit a snag,

30

silently accepted the idiot boy's company. Gjelosh gazed at him in adoration and shoved away anyone who got too close to the man's scribbles in the sand; he uttered not a sound in the man's presence. His tongue was unleashed only when the designer returned to his hut. "Eh, Gjelosh," people said, "Tell us how your master works." And Gjelosh would be delighted to seize a stick and scribble in the ground so furiously that mud and pebbles flew twenty paces off. "That's how," he went, frantically scratching the ground.

10

THE ENGINEER left just as he had arrived, unseen by anyone. One morning Gjelosh the idiot was to be seen scurrying around the hut, once again padlocked. He pressed his nose to the cracks, peered inside for a long time, and then went ambling round the hut again. He apparently could not believe that the man was no longer there, and so was looking for some other hole or chink in order to find him.

This went on almost all day. Never had the idiot's eyes looked so disconsolate.

II

THE RAFT continued to punt men and livestock across the Ujana e Keqe. I do not know why, but after the decision to build the bridge I began to keep an eye on what sort of traffic went to and fro across the river by raft. On the last Saturday in March, I spent almost the entire day near the old jetty watching the traffic. The weather was cold, with a thin rain that erased from the sandbank the final traces of the departed engineer's scrawls. People sat miserably on the raft, huddled against the cold, trying to turn their backs to the bitter wind. The expressions on their pinched faces gave little clue as to why they were crossing the river. Maybe they were travelling for their health, or to pay a call, or they might just be on their way to the bank, or to a funeral. Almost half the faces among them were familiar, while the others were utter strangers, and it was quite useless to attempt to discover who they might be. A monk's habit or the cloak of a simple icon-seller might conceal the Venetian envoy on a secret mission. Such things were known to have happened.

12

THREE DAYS later, I watched the raft again from the porch of the parish house. Only two goatherds with their few animals were crossing. The ferry made the journey several times to carry the entire herd across. The herdsmen were wrapped in cloaks like those of all common shepherds, but their tall pointed caps made them look somehow frightening from a distance.

Another day at dawn, I heard through my sleep some distant voices, apparently calling for help, and shouting "*Ujk, ujk . . .*" – "Wolf, wolf!" I leaped out of bed and strained an ear: lingering cries of "Uk, oh U-u-uk." I went outside and in the dim dawn light I made out four or five people on the opposite bank round a big black chest. They were calling the ferryman. I could barely capture their shouts, stretching like a film over the swollen waters of the river. It was a cold, bleak morning, and who knows what had prompted them to set out on their road before dawn? "Uk, oh U-u-uk," they called to the ferryman, holding their palms round their mouths like the bells of trumpets.

Finally I saw the bowed figure of Uk on his way down to the bank no doubt muttering curses under his breath at these unknown travellers, the raft, the river, and himself.

When the raft drew near the opposite bank and the travellers boarded, I saw that the black object was nothing less than a coffin, which they carefully lifted onto the planks of the raft.

I went back to bed to rest a while longer, but sleep eluded me.

13

T<small>HE</small> F<small>IRST</small> contingent of men and laden mules arrived
at midday on the seventeenth of April. At their head
strode Gjelosh, waving his arms as if he were pounding a
drum, and puffing out his cheeks as though trumpeting: he
was beside himself with joy.

The men and mules halted on the riverbank, right beside
the engineer's empty hut. There, in the waste land among
the wild burdocks, they started unloading. This took all day.
By late afternoon, the riverbank was unrecognizable. It was
a complete jumble; people scurried about, speaking some
thorny hybrid tongue, amid the piles of planks, ladders,
creeper-like ropes, stakes, cleats, and implements of every
kind. There was so much hubbub that even Gjelosh was
taken aback, and I rather suspect that his high spirits were
dampened.

Late that evening, the new arrivals began building sheds
by torchlight. That night some of them slept in the open,
if such perpetual restlessness could be called sleep. They
groaned in their sleep, kept getting up and wandering
aimlessly from the bushes to the riverbank, calling to each
other at the tops of their voices and seeming to sing, weep,
or groan in their sleep. They sang, wept, hooted like owls,
and threw up exactly over the spot where the toads were.
In the fitful torchlight everything took on the appearance

of a nightmare. In fact, the anxiety and sleeplessness they brought with them were the first impression they conveyed to those around them. The construction of storage sheds and dormitories went on for several days. It was surprising to see how even such rickety huts could emerge from this clutter. The disorder looked incapable of resolving itself into anything, and as for a bridge coming out of it, that seemed quite incredible. These road people were as uncouth and chaotic as the "Ferries and Rafts" people were meticulous and organized in everything they did.

By the end of April, two further caravans arrived, but work on the actual bridge did not begin until the headman came, or the foreman as they called him, because it seemed that he himself would direct the building of the bridge. Excavations began a long way from the water, and to one side by the bushes, as if the bridge were to run off in that direction, as far from the river as possible. They opened all kinds of pits and dead-end ditches. Everybody laboured to level the ground, far away from the water, almost as if they wanted to delude the river: "We have nothing to do with you. Can't you see how far away we're digging? Flow on in peace."

The network of pits and trenches seemed to have less and less connection with any plan. People began to think that the foreman was quite simply a little weak in the head, and was frittering away the money allotted for the construction of the bridge. They even said it was no accident that Gjelosh made friends with him so quickly. It takes one to know one.

Of course, Gjelosh scampered about all day amidst the confusion, puffing out his cheeks, gnashing his teeth, and pretending to beat a drum. Nobody shooed him away. Even the foreman's two assistants who were supervising the work said nothing to him. In contrast to their master, they were garrulous and were to be found everywhere. One of them was powerfully built, bald, and with abscesses on his throat, which some people said were signs of an incurable disease, while others insisted that they were scars from the torture he had been subjected to in an attempt to extract his bridge-building secrets from him. Those of this second persuasion were again split into two camps. The one said that he had caved in and divulged his secret, and others claimed that he had endured everything they could do, arching his back like a bridge under his sufferings, and had told his enemies nothing.

The second assistant on the other hand was scrawny; everything about him was thin and angular – his head, chin, and forearms. Later, when they often waded into the river mud, they said that the foreman always turned his back on him as they talked in order not to have to see his horrible shins.

WHEN THE heat tightened its hold and the Ujana e
Keqe subsided considerably, work suddenly intensi-
fied round the network of ditches flanking the river. The
labourers extended the trenches one by one as far as the bank
itself, and then joined them to the river, whose water now
began to flow into them. Seen from above, the channels
resembled great leeches, sucking the water from the already
enfeebled river.

It took less than two days for the appearance of the Ujana
e Keqe to change completely. In place of the gentle shimmer
of the waters, thick mud spread everywhere, with a few dull
glints here and there.

Further downstream the channels led the water back to the
river again, but on the site of the bridge everything was disfigured and bedraggled. Dead fish lay scattered in the mud.
Turtles and diver-birds gave a final glimmer before perishing.
Wandering bards, arriving from who knows where, looked
glumly at the wretched spectacle of the river and muttered:
"What if some naiad or river nymph has died? What will
happen then?"

The old raft was moved a short distance downstream and
the hunchbacked ferryman spent all day cursing the newcomers who tramped ceaselessly back and forth through
the bog with buckets of mud that left them so filthy they

looked like ghosts. Now not only the river but the whole surrounding area became smeared with mud. Its traces extended as far as the main road, or even further still, as far as the Inn of the Two Roberts.

The lugubrious, unsociable foreman wandered to and fro amid the chaos of the building site. As protection from the· sun he wore on his head not a straw hat like anybody else but a visor that shielded only his eyes. Sometimes, against the general muddiness, the rays of the evening sun seemed to strike devilish sparks from his carrot top. People no longer said he was mad; now he was the only sane man in a crowd of madmen, and the question was whether he would be able to keep this demented throng in harness.

As time passed, the river became an eyesore. It looked like a squashed eel, and you could almost imagine that it would shortly begin to stink. Regardless of all the damage it had caused, people began to feel sorry for it.

Old Ajkuna wept to see it. "How could they kill the river?" she cried. "How could they flay it alive!" She wept for it as if it had been a living person. "Killed in its sleep, poor creature! Caught defenceless and hacked to pieces!"

She climbed down into the mud to seek out the engineer. "The day will come when the river takes its revenge," she muttered. "It will fill with water and be strong again. It will swell and roar. And where will you hide then? Where?"

Whenever she thought she spied the foreman in the distance, she would raise her stick threateningly: "Where will you hide then, Antichrist!"

15

WHILE THEY were still digging the pits for the foundations of the bridge piers, our liege lord, the Count of the Gjikas, received a request for his daughter's hand in marriage. The request was very unusual. It came from none of the Albanian or European dukes, barons, and princes, as might have been expected, but from a direction whence betrothals and wedding guests had never come before, the Turkish state. The governor of one of the empire's border provinces asked for the count's daughter for his son Abdullah (what a dreadful name!). The proposal, as the envoys said, was made with the knowledge of the sultan-emperor, so it was not difficult to realize that this was a political match. Our liege lord, Stres Gjikondi, had been aloof towards his new neighbours, and now they were trying to mollify him.

For longer than people could remember, betrothals had been like a calming oil poured on the troubled waters of hostility and division among the nobles of Arberia. Of course these things pacified matters for a time, but not for long. If there was a recent excuse for a coolness, people's minds worried at it, until the day of the unpalatable announcement came, "We have important business." As to what came after, people knew that well enough: a fracas.

A year earlier, the Count of Kashnjet had asked for the hand of our liege lord's only daughter, and immediately afterwards so had the duke of the Gjin family, or Dukagjin as he is called for short, whose arms carry a single-headed white eagle. But our liege lord did not grant his daughter to her first suitor for reasons known only to himself, while the second withdrew his suit after an ambush by persons unknown at the Poplar Copse, doubtless suborned precisely for this task by those old enemies of our count, the Skuraj family, whose princely arms carry in the centre a wolf with bared teeth.

For the last hundred years quarrels among the Albanian princes and lords have been frequent to the point of despair. The Balsha family, princes of the north, whose arms carry a six-pointed white star and who in recent years have been in continual financial straits, could seldom agree with the haughty Topia family, who lay claim to the throne of all Arberia. Nor have the Balshas been on good terms with the counts of Myzeqe, the Muzakas, who have added to their old arms a forked stream which is rumoured to suggest the springs of oil recently discovered on their lands. Yet the Muzakas likewise have been almost continually at odds with Aranit Komneni, the powerful prince of Vlora, even though both families are allied by marriage to the emperors of Byzantium, in contrast to the Dukagjins, Balshas, and Topias, who have forged their marriage alliances abroad, exclusively with the French royal family. Nor have the Muzakas been on good terms with the Kastriotis, whose arms also bear an eagle, though not a white one like the Dukagjins' but a red one with two heads. People say that the dukes of Gjin are descended from the marriage long ago of the chieftain Gjin to a mountain nymph, while the Kastrioti family, or Castriothi, as they sometimes write their name, are the only Albanian lords to use antique pearls for seals. Two years earlier, there would have been a general slaughter among the men of Dukagjin and the Kastriotis at the wedding of the Count of Kashnjet, had it not been for the intervention of Dejdamina, the old dowager.

The lords of Arberia imagined they could settle these quarrels by marriages. But, as I mentioned, these alliances thrown across this stormy sea have been merely like rainbows straining to climb a few degrees above the abyss. The marriages of the great Count Topia with Katrina, the sister of Balsha II, of the latter with Komita, daughter of the Prince of Vlora, and that of the younger brother, Gjergj Balsha, to Marija, the daughter of Andre Muzaka, did not in the least prevent the three venerable princely houses from very soon setting aside the wedding lutes for the drums of war.

Marriages with foreigners have not been any more successful. Ever since the Albanian prince Tanush Topia, father of the present Count Karl Topia, snatched Hélène d'Anjou, daughter of the King of France, from the French escorts who were accompanying her to her wedding in Byzantium, ill fortune has dogged many of the marriages in the land of Arberia. In kidnapping the French princess, Tanush Topia was quite heedless of the fact that he was making enemies of both France and Byzantium, both states far more powerful than his. He lived with the French-woman for five years, and she bore him two children. His father-in-law, the king of France, pretended to forget the offence, and invited the couple, son-in-law and bride, to Paris, supposedly for a reconciliation. He killed them both and still today, after so many years, whenever I see the Topia arms with its lion crowned with the white lilies of the Angevins, it reminds me of a tombstone.

Aranit Komneni's marriage into the imperial house of

Byzantium was no less troubled. However, where Tanush Topia's marriage became the cause of a quarrel, here, on the contrary, a quarrel was extinguished by a marriage. Aranit Komneni's coolness with Byzantium arose over the old naval base of Orikum near Vlora. Taking advantage of Byzantium's awkward situation, the Albanian prince brought to light some old documents proving that, before it had been captured and rebuilt by Rome, Orikum had belonged to Illyria, that is the Arberia of today. Without waiting for the conclusion of diplomatic negotiations with the empire, he attacked and captured one-half of the base, which was defended by a garrison of Scandinavian mercenaries. Byzantium then hurried to offer him a princess as a wife, in order to preserve at least joint possession of the base and the small private beaches – the emperor's property – nearby. They say that the Turks have recently been doing their utmost to persuade Komneni to hand the base over to them. They have promised the aged prince fabulous sums, and even a princess for his son, if he will cede to them at least his own portion of the base, in other words one-half. Rumour has it that Aranit has insisted that he will not exchange the base for the most beautiful girl on earth, because, he says, the base is the most beautiful girl on land or sea alike.

Turks have been appearing increasingly often all over the Balkans. You meet them on the highways, at inns, at city gates waiting for permission to enter, at fairs, on the ferries, all over the place. Sometimes they turn up under political or commercial auspices, sometimes as trade missions, sometimes as groups of wandering musicians, adherents of religious sects, military units, or as solitary eccentrics. Increasingly often you hear their attenuated melodies, heavy with somnolence. Everything about them makes me anxious, their manners, their supple gait, and the hidden movements inside their loose garments that seem especially created to conceal the vigour of their limbs, and above all their language: their words, in contrast to their drowsy songs, end with a crack like a blow from a mallet. This is something different from the conflicts so far. My anxiety turns to pure terror when I think of all that these people are concealing. There is something deceitful in their smiles and courtesy. It is no accident that their silken garments, turbans, breeches, and robes have no straight lines, corners, hems, or seams. Their whole costume is insubstantial, and cut in a way to change its shape continually. Among such diaphanous folds it is hard to tell whether a hand is holding a knife or a flower. But after all, what is to be expected from a people who hide their very origins: their women?

Some time ago, I happened to see one of their military units on its homeward journey after taking part in the conflict between the barons of Ohri and the Muzakas. It was a body of mercenaries who had been under contract to fight for a fixed period and a fixed fee. The Albanian princes, like those elsewhere in the Balkans and the Byzantine emperors themselves, have for some years been calling on Turkish units for use in their their internecine squabbles. This was how they first appeared in the Balkan lands. My flesh crept when I saw them travelling in formation along the highway with that sombre gait that armies have the world over. They are leaving us, I thought, but taking us with them. Their eyes roved covetously about, and I remembered the saying of my father Gjorg that every invasion starts in the eyes.

Who first called them in? I fear that many peoples of Europe will one day be asking this question. It will be not a question, but a shriek. And no one will answer it. It will be not a question but a cry of agony. And no one will have the answer. Everyone will try to shift the blame. The truth is already becoming shrouded in mist. Almost as if it were wrapped in Turkish silk.

And that is where this marriage proposal was coming from. When the Ottoman envoys crossed the river by raft, laden with expensive gifts, to visit the count, they were all charm. Their ample breeches whispered with the stealthy swish of silk. On their return, however, they looked black as thunder. The henna glowed threateningly on their short beards. Our liege lord had refused to grant them his daughter. To avoid making matters worse, he had given her young age as an excuse, and her delicate state of health. In fact the girl was seventeen and, although her sickness had left her rather pale, she was now completely cured. But it was clear that this alliance was the last thing the count wanted.

16

ALL THAT summer, day and night, the work of erecting the bridge piers continued. They dug pits for the foundations until they struck bedrock, and then began filling them with large stones. These were brought by cart from an old, distant quarry, and were lowered into the pits with the help of a great winch. Its squeaking did not cease day or night, as it lowered stones slung from stout rope, and buckets filled with mortar.

Lime pits had been dug nearby, and some of the men working on the bridge piers were entirely coated with white. But mud remained the predominant colour.

The foreman with his assistants spent hours on the wooden scaffolding that surrounded each of the pits. Sometimes they swarmed like demons all over the cross-nailed timbers and sometimes, when the heat overcame them, they would plunge stark naked into the river, and never mind what anyone thought. They worked tirelessly in order to raise the piers before autumn came, when the Ujana e Keqe would swell. The diversion channels were intended only for the dry season, and after the first rains they would be unable to cope with the volume of water, part of which would flow again in the old bed.

Whenever a cloud appeared in the sky, the foreman lifted his carrot head towards the mountains with an anxious look.

In fact, everybody was waiting for autumn to come. Some were curious to see what the river would do when it met the obstacles in its path. Others shook their heads, convinced that the Ujana e Keqe would know how to exact its revenge. Not for nothing was it called the Accursed Ujana.

People waited for the river to rise, in the way that they wait for someone who has been away from home for a long time, while great changes have taken place in his absence. Although most took the side of the river, and even laid wagers on the scale of its revenge, there were also those who felt pity for the bridge. However, they were still few and they concealed their sympathy.

The days were drawing in. Summer gave way to autumn without anything noteworthy happening. A workman drowned in a lime pit, and two others were crippled by the winch, but these were very minor incidents compared with what had been expected.

17

NOT ONLY the Cassandras , who always crop up on the eve of disasters, but everyone was in a state of fever. One day towards the middle of the first month of autumn, the river was more turbulent than usual. There had been a storm somewhere in the mountains.

The new waters surged forward like the vanguard of an army, but the diversion channels swallowed them with ease, not letting them flood the works.

It was now clear that the confrontation between the river and the bridge builders was at hand.

Some clear days went by, and then the skies clouded over. A thin, penetrating drizzle fell that seemed determined not to leave an inch of the world dry. Wrapped in sleeveless black cloaks, the labourers pressed on dauntlessly with their work under the rain. "Why are they not afraid?" people said. "How can their legs keep them there, now that the river is waking from its sleep?"

Yet the river seemed to bide its time, collecting its strength before attacking.

The diversion channels barely coped with one new onrush of water. But the Ujana e Keqe still did not show its mettle. Old Ajkuna said that the river would play with the bridge like a cat with a mouse.

Several more days of rain passed, and now the river's delay

was more alarming than any onslaught. Even the builders themselves, cool-headed so far, seemed to grow anxious. A few cold and distant flashes of lightning, like mute heralds, added to the terror. It has sent every sign, people said. Woe to those who fail to realize that.

The river's attack was expected daily, even hourly, but still it did not come. "Oh, not for nothing is it called the Accursed," people said. "It has never been short of tricks."

And indeed it came when no one expected it. After the days of rain, the weather unexpectedly cleared. The sky above was blue, blinding the eyes, and nobody thought that the river, which had been so well behaved during the days of rain, could attack now. But that is precisely the time it chose to strike.

First a roar was heard, like a thunderclap, and suddenly the waters were unleashed. In a furious onslaught they over-flowed the diversion channels and surged into their old bed. In moments everything was laid waste, pits and clay-packed dykes vanished in the twinkling of an eye. The waters made trash of the planks, beams, pulleys, sieves, and general debris, which were thrown all over the place, and then with redoubled force hurled themselves against the unfinished stone piers. They carried with them not only tree stumps and stones, but goats, wolves, and even drowned snakes that resembled the emblems and terrifying symbols of an army. They stormed the bridge head-on, were repulsed, lunged from the left, poured in from the right, and foamed wildly below the piers. But the stone piers took no notice. Only then did people notice the foreman still poised on top of the planks connecting the two piers, studying the angry surge of the Ujana e Keqe. Now and then he would laugh, so people claimed.

It was clear that the Ujana e Keqe had failed in its first contest with the stone yoke they were casting over it. The debris it carried down, along with a drunken mason snatched by the flood, were not much of a revenge. The water surged on, wilder than ever, and the Ujana e Keqe, coloured by the clay it carried, seemed stained with blood.

People looked at the stone teeth planted in the water, and pitied the river. It will rise again, they said; it will recover from its summer sickness and then we'll see what havoc it wreaks.

But two weeks passed, the river rose still higher, its waves grew stronger, and its roar grew deeper, but still it did no damage to the bridge.

18

THE SECOND month of autumn was cold as seldom before. After the first flood, the waters of the Ujana e Keqe cleared and reverted to their usual colour, between pale blue and green. But this colour, familiar to us for years, now seemed to conceal cold fury and outrage. The labourers, laden with stones and buckets of mortar, moved like fiends among the planks and beams connecting the piers. The river flowed below, minding its own business, while the workmen above minded theirs.

Throughout October nothing of nóte occurred. A drowned corpse, brought by the waters from who knows where, collided with the central pier, spun round it a while, and vanished again. It was on that very day that there dimly emerged from among the mass of scaffolding and nailed crossbeams something like an arc connecting the two central piers. Apparently they were preparing to set in place the first arch.

19

O N THE threshold of winter, along with the first frosts, wandering dervishes turned up everywhere. They were seen along the high road, by the Inn of the Two Roberts, and further away, by the Fever Stone. Travellers arriving from neighbouring principalities said that they had seen them there too, and some even said that Turkish dervishes had been seen along the entire length of the old Via Egnatia. Sometimes in small groups or in pairs, but in most cases alone, they ate up the miles with their bare muddy feet.

Early yesterday morning, I saw two of them walking with that nimble gait of theirs along the deserted road. One led the way, the other followed two paces behind, and I looked at their rags, so soiled by the dust and the winter wind, and asked almost aloud, "Why?"

Who are these vagrants, and why have they appeared throughout the peninsula at the same time, on this threshold of winter?

20

FROST COVERED the ground. Two wandering bards had stayed three consecutive nights at the Inn of the Two Roberts, entertaining the guests with new ballads. The ballads had been composed on the subject of the Ujana e Keqe and were inauspicious. What you might call their content was more or less as follows: the naiads and water nymphs would never forget the insult offered to the Ujana e Keqe. Revenge might be slow, but come it would.

Such ballads would be very much to the taste of the people from "Ferries and Rafts". Yet now that they had lost their battle and the bridge was being built, not one and not a thousand ballads could help them, because so far no-one has heard of songs destroying a bridge or a building of any kind.

Since their final departure, defeated and despondent, the "Ferries and Rafts" people had been seen no more. They seemed vanished from the face of the earth but now the ballads at the Inn of the Two Roberts brought them back to mind. Had they given up the fight, or were they biding their time?

Meanwhile the Ujana e Keqe looked more askance at us than ever, or perhaps so it seemed to us because we knew of the yoke of stone on its neck.

21

As the season drew to an end, our liege lord invited distinguished guests to a hunt in the Wolf's Wilderness, as he did every year at about the same time.

The neighbouring lords and vassals came, and so did Gjin Bue Shpata, the powerful overlord of southern Arberia. The two sons of old Balsha, Gjergj Balsha and Balsha II, came from the north together with their wives, the countesses Marija and Komita. They were followed by the lord of Zadrima, Nikollë Zaharia, whose arms bear a lynx, and the barons Pal Gropa, lord of Ohri and Pogradec, and Vlash Matranga, lord of Karavasta, as well as another lord, whose name was kept secret and who was said only to be a "man of note in the Great Mountains".

As in every other year , the hunt was conducted with all the proper splendour. Hunting horns, horses' hooves, and the pack of hounds kept the whole of Wolf's Wilderness awake a full day and night. No accidents occurred, apart from the death of a beater who was mauled by a bear; Nikollë Zaharia sprained his ankle, which particularly worried the nobility, but this passed quickly.

The good weather held. At the end of the hunt, there was a powdering of snow and the snow-dusted procession of hunters on their homeward journey looked all the more attractive.

Nevertheless, as I watched them in their ordered progress a spasm seized my soul. The emblems and signs on the noblemen's jerkins, those wild goats' horns, eagles' wings, and lions' manes involuntarily reminded me of the drowned animals that the Ujana e Keqe had so ominously carried down to the gorge. Defend our princes, o Lord, I silently prayed. Holy Mary, avert the evil hour.

The guests did not stay long, because they were all anxious to return to their own lands. During the three days that they stayed in all (less than ever before), we expected news of some new betrothal, but no such thing occurred. In fact, the guests discussed in secret the situation created by the Ottoman threat.

While these discussions continued, the two countesses, the sisters-in-law Marija and Komita, asked to visit the bridge site. It fell to me to escort them and to give them an outline of the phases in the building of the bridge, about which they had no idea. They were impressed for a while by the swarm of workmen that teemed on the sand, by the melee, the din, and the different languages spoken. Then Komita, who had been visiting her father in Vlora a month before, mentioned the anxiety over the Orikum naval base, and then they had a lot to say about their acquaintances in great houses, especially the Duchess of Durrës, Johana, who was preparing to remarry after the death of her husband, and so on and so forth, finally arriving at their sister-in-law Katrina, the darling daughter of old Balsha, of whom they were obviously jealous. I attempted to bring the conversation back to the Orikum base, but it was extremely difficult, not to say impossible.

Under our feet, the Ujana e Keqe roared on with its greyish crests, but neither the river nor the bridge could hold their attention any further. They went on gossiping about their acquaintances, their love affairs, and their precious jewellery; try as I might not to listen, something of their chatter penetrated my ears. For a while they disparaged the Ottoman governor's proposal of marriage to the daughter of our count. They dissolved in laughter over what they called their "Turkish bridegroom", imagining his baggy breeches; they held on to each other so as not to fall into the puddles in their mirth. Then, amid fresh gales of laughter, they tried to pronounce his name, "Abdullah", saying it ever more oddly, especially when they tried to add an affectionate diminutive "th" to the end.

22

AFTER MICHAELMAS and during the first week of winter, we still saw dervishes everywhere. It struck me that these horrible vagabonds could only be the scouts of the great Asiatic state that destiny had made our neighbour.

They were no doubt gathering information about the land, the roads, the alliances or quarrels among the Albanian princes, and their old disputes. Sometimes, when I saw them, it struck me that it was easier to collect quarrels under the freezing December wind than at any other time.

I was involuntarily reminded of snatches of the conversation between the two dainty countesses, and I would sometimes find myself, without knowing why, muttering to myself like an idiot the name of the "Turkish bridegroom": Abdullahth.

23

ONE OF the deacons attached to the parish woke me to tell me that something had happened by the bridge. Even though he had gone as far as the riverbank himself, he had been unable to find out anything precisely.

I jumped out of bed immediately. As often when I heard disturbing news or had a dream, I instinctively turned my head towards the mountains. This was a habit from childhood, when my grandmother used to say to me: "Any sign you may receive, for good or ill, you must first tell it to the mountains."

One could sense that it was snowing in the mountains, although they themselves were invisible. When we arrived at the riverbank, the sight was indeed incredible. As the deacon had told me, the builders had stopped work, a thing that had never happened before. Those whom neither sleet nor hail, nor even the Ujana e Keqe itself, had succeeded in driving from the bridge, had left their work half-done and were scattered in groups on the sandbank, some looking towards the bridge, and some towards the river, as if they had never seen them before.

As we drew closer, I noticed other people who had clambered on to the scaffolding and perched on the beams like vultures. Among them I recognized the foreman and his two assistants. They were crouched by the stone arch, saying something to one another, bending down to study the piers, then huddling together once more to resume their discussion.

"Gjelosh, what's happened?" someone asked the idiot, who was hurrying away from the site.

"The bridge, br, bad, very bad, bridge, pa, pa, fright," he answered.

A few hours later we learned the truth: the bridge had been damaged in several places during the night. Several almost inexplicable crevices, like scratches made by claws, had appeared in the central piers, the approach arches, and especially on the newly-completed span. As pale as wax, the foreman's assistants tried to imagine what kind of tools could have done such damage. The foreman, wrapped in his cloak, stared frostily at the horizon, as if the answer might come from there.

"But these aren't marks made by tools, sir," one of the masons said at last.

"What?" the foreman said.

"These aren't hammer marks, or chisel marks, or . . ."

"Well then, what are they?" the foreman asked.

The mason shrugged his shoulders and looked round at the others. Their faces were ashen.

"At the Inn of the Two Roberts, a few weeks ago," one of them muttered, "the bards said something about naiads and water nymphs . . ."

"That's enough of that," the foreman yelled, and abruptly crouched again by the damaged arch to study the cracks. He studied them for a long time, and when he too saw that they really did not look like marks made by hammers, picks, or crowbars, he too shivered in terror like the rest.

24

THE NEWS that the bridge had been damaged led folk to appear on both banks of the Ujana, just as in the days after the flood, when everybody hurried to collect tree stumps for firewood.

The surface of the waters was now a blank. People watched for hours on end, and there were those who swore that they had discerned beneath the waves, if not naiads themselves, at least their tresses or their reflections. They then recalled the wandering bards, remembered their clothes and faces, and especially strove to recall the words of their ballads, distorting their rhymes, as when the wind bends the tops of reeds.

"Who would have thought their songs would come true?" they said thoughtfully. "They weren't singers, they were wizards."

The Ujana e Keqe meanwhile flowed on obliviously. It had been damaged and torn since its unsuccessful onslaught, so that in places it was no more than a gully, but it had not given up. It had finally succeeded in crippling the bridge.

At night, the bridge lifted blackly over the river its solitary span, which they had so cruelly wounded. From a distance, the mortar and fresh lime of the repaired patches resembled rags tied round a broken limb. In its injured state the bridge looked positively weird.

25

JUST AT this time, for two successive nights, a strange monk named Brockhardt stayed with us on his way back to Europe from Byzantium, where he had been sent on his country's service.

I was reading in the last of the daylight when I had word that a person who seemed to be a monk had crossed the river on the last raft and was asking questions in some incomprehensible tongue. I gave orders for him to be brought to me.

He was tall, gaunt, emaciated, and dressed in amazingly dust-covered clothes.

"I have never seen such a long road," he said, pointing to himself with his finger, as if his journey weighed on his body like a yoke. "And almost the whole of it under repair."

I studied his muddied appearance with some surprise and hastened to excuse it.

"It is the old Via Egnatia, which a highway maintenance company is repairing," I said.

He nodded and removed his cloak, releasing a cloud of dust. "The same people as are building this stone bridge."

"Yes," he said. "I saw it as I arrived."

He looked even lankier without his cloak. His limbs were

so scrawny, that if he had crossed his arms, mere skin and bone, he would have resembled a death's head.

"There's a spur from the road to the military base at Vlora, isn't there?" he said.

He must be a spy, I thought.

"Yes," I replied.

After all, what did it matter to me if he asked about the Vlora base? It belonged to somebody else now.

I invited him to sit down on the soft rug by the fire and laid out the low table.

"Sit down and we will eat. You must be hungry."

I uttered these words somewhat tentatively, as if I was unsure of being able to satisfy the appetite of so skeletal a person. He seemed to have read my mind, for he grinned and whispered into my ear:

"I am a guest. The Slavs say *gost*, and have derived this from the English word ghost." He smiled. "But, like every soul alive, I need meat, ha-ha-ha!"

He laughed in a way that looked positively scary. I tried not to watch his Adam's apple, which seemed to be about to come clean out of his throat.

"Help yourself. Make yourself at home," I said.

He went on chuckling for a while, not lifting his eyes from the table. The thought that I had the opportunity to spend the evening with a man who knew something about language gave me a thrill of pleasure.

"And what is the news out there?" I asked, saving the subject of languages for later.

He spread his arms, as if to say: Nothing special.

"In Europe, you know, war has been going on for a hundred years," he said. "And Byzantium seethes with schemes and plots."

"As always," I said.

"Yes. As always. They have just finished celebrating the anniversary of the defeat of the Bulgarian army and its blinding. Since then, everybody seems to have lost their heads. As you may know, that is a country that is always on the look-out for excitement."

"The blinding of the Bulgarian army? What was that?"

"Don't you know?" he said. "It was a terrible thing, and they solemnly celebrate it every year."

Brockhardt told me briefly about the Byzantine emperor's punishment of the defeated Bulgarian army. Fifteen thousand captured Bulgarian soldiers had had their eyes put out. (You know that is a recognized punishment in Byzantium, he said). Only one hundred and fifty were left with their sight intact, to lead the blind army back to the Bulgarian capital. Day and night, their faces pitted with black holes, the blind hordes made their way homeward.

"Horrible," said Brockhardt, swallowing a large chunk of meat. "Don't you think?"

It seemed to me that the more he ate, instead of putting on flesh, as he had jokingly said, the thinner and paler he became.

"Great powers take a great revenge," he said.

We talked for a while about politics. He shared my opinion that Byzantium was in decline and that the main threat of our time came from the Turkish state.

"At every inn where I stopped," he said, "people talked of nothing else."

"And no doubt everybody indulged in vain guesswork over who had first brought them out of their wilderness, and nobody has the least idea how to stop the flood."

"That is right," said Brockhardt. "When people are not inclined to fight an evil, they limit themselves to speculating on its cause. But these Turks are an imminent danger for you too, aren't they?"

"Yes, they are on our doorstep."

"Ah yes, you are where Europe begins."

He asked about our country and it was apparent at once that his knowledge about it was hazy. I told him that we are the descendants of the Illyrians and that the Latins call our country Arbanum or Albanum or Regnum Albaniae, and call the inhabitants Arbanenses or Albanenses, which is the same thing. Then I told him that in recent years a new name for our country has grown up among the people themselves. This new name is Shqipëria, which comes from *shqiponjë*, meaning "eagle". And so, our Arberia has recently become known as Shqipëria, which means a flight or community or union of eagles, and the inhabitants are known as *shqiptarë*, from the same word.

He listened to me closely and I went on to explain to him a Serbian list of names of peoples, with totemic features, that a Slovene monk had shown me. In it, the Albanians were characterized as eagles (*dobar*), the Huns as rabbits, the Serbs as wolves, the Croats as owls, the Magyars as lynxes, and the Romanians as cats.

He nodded continually and, when I told him that we Albanians, together with the Greeks, are the oldest people in the Balkans, he thoughtfully raised his spoon. "We have had our roots here," I continued, "since time immemorial. The Slavs, who have recently become so embittered, as often happens with newcomers, arrived from the steppes of the east no more than three or four centuries ago."

I knew that I would have to demonstrate this to him some-how, and so I talked to him about the Albanian language, and told him that, according to some of our monks, it is contemporary with if not older than Greek, and that this, the monks say, was proved by the words that Greek had borrowed from our tongue.

"And they are not just any words," I said, "but the names of gods and heroes."

His eyes sparkled. I told him that the words "Zeus," "Dhemetra", "Tetis", and "Odhise", and "Kaos", according to our monks, stemmed from the Albanian words *zë*, for "voice", *dhe* for "earth", *det* for "sea", *udhë* for "journey", and *haes* for "eater". He laid down his spoon.

"Eat, ghost," I said, staring almost apprehensively at his spoon, which seemed to be the only tool binding him to the world of the living.

"These are amazing things you are telling me."

"When someone borrows your words for gods, it is like borrowing a part of your soul," I said after a pause. "But never mind, this is no time for useless boasting. Now, the Ottoman language is casting its shadow over both our languages, Greek and Albanian, like a black cloud."

He nodded.

"Wars between languages," he said, "are no less tragic than wars between men."

I was sorry to have brought up the topic.

"The language of the East is drawing nearer," I repeated after a while. We looked deep into each other's eyes. "With its '-*luk*' suffix," I went on slowly. "Like some dreadful hammer blow."

"Woe betide you," he said.

I shook my head in despair.

"And nobody recognizes the danger," I said.

"Ah," he said, and with a sudden movement, as if freeing himself from a snare, he rose from the table.

Now he was free to become a ghost again.

26

THREE DAYS after Brockhardt left, the bridge was damaged again. This time it was no longer a matter of cracks and scratches; some stones in its central piers had been removed. The strangest thing was that some of these stones were dislodged from beneath the surface of the water, and this, apart from adding to people's terror, caused great trouble to the builders. It was almost impossible to carry out repairs at this point until the water level dropped again next summer.

This second intervention of the spirits of the water caused general alarm. Despite the rage of the foreman and his assistants (the engineer's head might appear like a bolt of lightning at any part of the bridge), the pace of work slackened at once. Instead of the mud from the building site, terrifying rumours now spread out from the sand of the riverbank, which now resembled some blighted plain. But these rumours spread faster and further than the mud.

Some of the workmen began to abandon their work. Clutching their bags, and even forgoing their wages, they stole away by night, considering the work site cursed.

Increasingly often, people in their interminable conversations began to voice the opinion that the bridge must be destroyed before it was too late.

27

THE FOREMAN himself suddenly vanished one morning before dawn. Nobody knew where he went or why; it seems that he himself had given no explanation. On the previous day he had lashed his two assistants with a hogshair whip (a thing he had never done before, so it was said), and accompanied the blows with all manner of insults: brazen liars, mangy curs, utter shits. Then he had tossed his whip into the river and was seen no more.

Work on the bridge proceeded more sluggishly than ever. Gjelosh wandered miserably round the foreman's hut, repeatedly putting his eye or ear to the keyhole. The foreman's assistants turned up here and there with the whip marks on their faces. One of them, the spindleshanks, was bitterly angry, as humiliated as a man could be by the marks of the lashes, while the other man, the stocky one, seemed pleased, and seized every opportunity to show off his welts, as proud of them as if they had been so many medals.

Meanwhile, in the absence of the foreman, work on the bridge grew quite disorganized. Everybody was convinced that he would never return again and that now nothing remained but the decision to pull down the bridge, or at least abandon it to the mercy of the waters.

But the foreman returned as unexpectedly as he had left. A group of officials accompanied him. As soon as they arrived they went to the site of the damage, which they surveyed for hours on end. They examined the scratches and the dislodged stones, shook their heads, and made incomprehensible gestures. One of them, to everybody's amazement, stripped off and dived into the water, apparently to inspect the damage below the water line.

The same thing happened the next day and the one after. The inspection team was headed by a tall, thin, extremely stooped man. He seemed to have some kind of cramp in his neck, because he could barely move his head. Judging by the respect shown to him by everybody, including even the foreman, who was no respecter of persons, it was assumed that he must be one of the principal proprietors of the highway and bridges company.

"Look how God has bent that cursed one double," said old Ajkuna when she saw him. "That's how he'll bend everyone who tries to build bridges. He'll bend them into arches like the bridges themselves, so that their heads touch their feet. Our forebears were right when they said, 'May you be bent double and eat your toes, you who stray from the path!'"

28

I WAS SUMMONED in haste to our count. Everyone was gathered there: the emissaries of the road owners, the foreman, and our liege lord's scribes. Their expressions were despondent. We waited for the count to arrive.

I could not at all imagine why this meeting was being held. Would there really be a decision to abandon the works? There was little chance of our liege lord handing back even a small percentage of the money he had received. They did not know his ways.

The delegation sat as if rooted to their high-backed seats. The stooped man who had been so powerfully cursed by old Ajkuna was among them.

These meetings were beginning to annoy me. So in particular was the road owners' garbled language, which made my head ache for two days after translating it. Both sides, the water people and the road people, were equally unknown to me, but at least the water people spoke clearly and precisely. But an hour's talk with the road people seemed to coat the table with the dust of their slovenly language, just as the building site was littered with their plaster.

I will do what I can today, I said to myself, but next time I simply must find an excuse to stay away.

The visitors glanced repeatedly at the door through which the count would enter. In fact, his delay could be construed as a reluctance to attend this meeting. The visitors seemed increasingly on tenterhooks. They stared into space, at their hands, or at some pieces of parchment scribbled with all kinds of sketches.

At last the count arrived. He nodded a frosty greeting, and sat down at the table.

"I'm listening," he said.

Evidently the tall, bent man was to speak first. He cleared his throat two or three times as if in search of the right pitch, and was about to say something, but then hesitated and seemed to abandon the idea.

"I'm listening," I translated for the count a second time.

The head of the deputation cleared his throat, and then drily observed:

"Certain people wish to destroy our bridge."

The count's eyebrows rose. They expressed surprise, but more expectation, and a hint of mockery.

"It is not the spirits of the water who are damaging our bridge, as rumour has it, but men," the visitor continued.

The count's face remained impassive.

The foreigners' representative studied the notes in front of him.

"We can tell you right away whom we suspect," he went on.

Our count shrugged his shoulders, as if to say that it was no concern of his whom they suspected. The visitor apparently misinterpreted the gesture, and hastened to add:

"Please do not misunderstand me. We don't suspect your own people in the least." He gulped. "Nor do we even suspect the Turks. Our suspicions lie elsewhere."

"I'm listening," said Stres Gjikondi for the third time.

72

The scratching of the quills of the count's two scribes made the silence even more vexing.

"The 'Ferries and Rafts' people are trying to bring down our bridge," said the foreigners' representative. His piercing eyes transfixed the count. His curved spine put even greater suspicion into his glare.

The count confronted his gaze calmly. It was obvious at once that he was barely interested in this matter. He had been worried all the time about the breach of relations with his Turkish neighbours and and he barely gave a thought to what was happening at the bridge.

"It is obvious that they have been and still remain opposed to the construction of bridges, because of reasons that may be imagined, in other words questions of profit," the foreigner continued. "They put forward the idea of destroying the bridge, and then they took action against it. With the help of paid bards, they spread the myth that the spirits of the water will not tolerate the bridge and that it must be destroyed."

His head, bent low over the table, turned left and right to gauge the impression his revelation made on us all. I believed him at once. In fact, I had suspected something of the sort before. If the bridge builders, whose representatives were here before us, could at the very start pay an epileptic and a wandering fortune-teller to be the first to advance the idea of building a bridge, then was it not possible that "Ferries and Rafts" could pay two wandering bards to spread the idea of its destruction?

"You must realize, my lord count," the foreigner went on, "that it is not the spirits of the water who cannot endure the bridge, but the grasping spirits of the directors of this gang of thieves called 'Ferries and Rafts'."

73

"Ha, ha!" the count laughed. "They say the same about you."

Small reddish spots appeared on the brow of the leader of the delegation.

"We have never sunk any of their ferries," he said. "Nor have we damaged any of their jetties."

"That is true," our liege lord said. "At least, I have never heard of such a thing."

"Nor will you," the other man interrupted. "But those others, my lord! You know yourself that they are doing their utmost to obstruct the building of this bridge. And when they saw they were not succeeding, or, in other words, when their despicable schemes were scotched by your lordship, they then produced the idea of destroying the bridge. First they placed their hopes in the fury of the river, but then, when nature did not help them, they sent their people to damage our bridge."

He paused again briefly, as if to let his audience take in what he said. It was clear, as I had suspected, that the water people would not give up the struggle easily. They were paying the road people back in their own coin. Apparently a battle over money was more savage than that fight between the crocodile and the tiger that the Netherlander had told me about.

"And that, my lord count, is where matters stand."

Our count stared on imperturbably at the stooped delegate. At last, when the man had apparently had his say, he spoke:

"So what do you want of me, gentlemen?"

The leader of the delegation fixed his gaze on the count's eyes once again, as if to say: Do you really not understand what we want?

"We want the culprits punished,"he said drily.

Our liege lord spread his arms. A bluish light filtered through the stained glass of the upper portion of the window, seeming to dissolve you and carry you far away. The count kept his arms open.

"It's no use asking that from me," he said finally. "I have never meddled in your business, and have no intention of doing so now."

"And are we to do the murder ourselves?"

"What?"

The pens of the scribes scratched disconsolately in the silence. The dim bluish light was by now quite oppressive.

"How do you mean, What?" said the leader of the delegation, hunched until his head was almost on the table.

The foreman's red head was opposite him, like a flame without heat.

"Did you mention a murder?" the count asked.

Their eyes were again fixed on each other.

"A punishment," the visitor said.

"Ah, yes, a punishment."

The silence continued after the scratching of the quills ceased, when any silence becomes unbearable.

Everybody expected the words of our liege-lord to fill this lull. His voice came, weary and indifferent, as if from beyond the grave.

"If it is true, as you say, that your enemies have hit upon the idea of destroying the bridge with the help of a myth, then you should devise some way of punishing the culprits in kind . . . in other words . . ."

The count left the phrase unfinished, which happened extremely rarely.

The strangers' eyes burned feverishly.

"I understand, my lord count," their leader said at last.

He raised his body from the seat, although his back and head remained hunched over the table, as if they could not be torn away. It was apparently not easy for him to move his back, and he remained thus for a very long time, while the others turned their heads towards the foreman, almost as if he, who knew the secrets of bridges, could help to lift that arched backbone.

The man finally succeeded in straightening up, and, after bidding the count farewell, the delegation filed out. I followed them.

It was cold outside. The north wind froze my ears. As I walked, I could not stop thinking of what they had talked about with the count. Something ominous had been discussed in a veiled way. Everything had been carefully shrouded. I had once seen the body of a murdered man on the main road, two hundred paces from the Inn of the Two Roberts. They had wrapped him in a cloth and left him there by the road. Nobody dared to lift the cloth to see the wounds. They must have been ghastly.

The thought that I had involuntarily taken part in a conspiracy to murder disturbed my sleep all night. My head was heavy next morning. Outside, everything was dismal. An age-old rain fell, heavy as iron. Oh God, I said to myself, what is the matter with me? And a wild desire seized me to weep, to weep heavy, useless tears, like this rain.

29

THE RAIN continued all that week, as drearily as on
that day of the discussion. People say that rain like
this falls once every four years. The heavens seemed to be
emptying the whole weight of the ages on to the earth.

In spite of the bad weather, work on the bridge did not
pause for a single day. Builders no longer abandoned the site.
Work on the second and third arches proceeded at speed.
Sometimes the mortar froze in the cold, and they were
obliged to mix it with hot water. Sometimes they threw salt
in the water.

The Ujana e Keqe swelled further and grew choppier, but
did not mount another assault on the bridge. It flowed
indifferently past it, disdainful and indifferent, and indeed,
to a foreign eye there was nothing here but an ordinary
bridge and river, like dozens of others, which had long ago
set aside the initial quarrels of living together and had made
their peace. However, if you looked carefully, you would see
that the Ujana e Keqe no longer reflected the bridge in its
waters. Or, if its furrows cleared and smoothed somewhat,
it only gave a blurred reflection, almost as if what loomed
above it were not a stone bridge but the fantasy or labour
of an unquiet spirit.

Everyone was waiting to see what the spirits of the
waters would get up to next. Water never forgets, the old

folk said. Earth is more generous, and forgets more quickly, but water never.

They said that the bridge was carefully guarded at night. The guards could not be seen anywhere, but no doubt they watched secretly from the scaffolding.

30

As soon as it had put its affairs in order, the deputation departed, leaving only one man behind. This was the quietest among them, a listless man with watery, colourless eyes. He kept himself to himself, as if not interfering in anyone's business, and he often walked quite alone by the riverbank. Gjelosh the idiot imagined – for reasons of his own – that he had a special right to threaten and insult this man whenever he saw him. The flaccid character observed the idiot's wild behaviour with surprise, and did his best to keep out of his way.

One day I happened to meet him face to face; he spoke to me first, apparently remembering me from the discussions with the count. We strolled a while together. He said that he was a collector of folk tales and customs. I wanted to ask what this had to do with the bridge but changed my mind. Perhaps it was those watery eyes that made me think better of it.

A few days later, he came to the parish house and we talked for a considerable time about Balkan tales and legends, some of which he knew. The surface of his tranquil gaze ruffled whenever I spoke of them, despite his attempts to control the stare of his somnolent eyes.

"Ever since I first heard of them, I can't wait to know more," he continued, as if by way of apology.

I recollected in a flash their delegation's interest in legends, and also how our count had mentioned them during the discussion. Now I no longer had any doubt that I really was talking to a collector of legends. And yet something deep down within me warned me to be on my guard. Some sort of summons or vision fought to reach my brain, but could not. I do not know what kind of fog prevented it.

"I hope I am not irritating you if I keep going over the same things," he continued.

"On the contrary," I said. "It is a pleasure for me. Like most of the monks in these parts, I myself take an interest in these matters."

As we walked along the riverbank, I explained to him that the legends and ballads of these parts mainly dealt with what had most distressed people throughout the ages, the division of mankind into the two tribes: the living and the dead. The maps and flags of the world witness to dozens of states, kingdoms, languages, and peoples, but in fact there are only two peoples, who live in two kingdoms: in this world, and in the next. In contrast to the petty kingdoms and statelets of our world, these great kingdoms have never touched each other, and this lack of contact has pained most of all the people on this side. No testimony, no message has so far ever come from the other side. Unable to endure this rift, this absence of a crossing, the people on this side have woven ballads against the barrier, dreaming of its destruction. Thus, these ballads mention those in the next world, in other words the dead, crossing to this side temporarily with the permission of their kingdom, for a short time, usually for one day, in order to redeem a pledge they have left behind or to keep a promise they have made.

"Ah, I see," he said now and then, while his eyes were begging me to continue.

I said that this is at least how we see it on this side. In other words, we are sure that the dead make efforts to reach us, but that is only our own point of view. Perhaps they think differently over there and if they heard our ballads would split their sides laughing . . .

"Ah, you think that they have little reason to want to come to us?"

"Nobody can know what they think," I replied. "Apart from Him above."

A few little birds, black ones that they call winter sparrows, flew about above our heads. He asked me whether all the ballads that were sung were old and I explained to him that sometimes new ones were devised, or rather, that is what people thought, whereas in fact all they did was to revive forgotten ones.

I told him that an incident in the neighbouring county ninety years ago, at the time of the first plague, had become the occasion for a new legend. A bride married into a distant house, and unable to explain her journey, had said that her dead brother had brought her home . . .

"Ah, it seems to me that I have heard it," he interrupted me. "A bride called Jorundina, if I am not mistaken."

"Jorundina or Doruntina. We pronounce it both ways."

"It is a heavenly ballad. Especially the suspicions against the young bride and her defence of herself by mentioning the promises her brother had made to her while he was alive . . . There is a special word in your language . . ."

"*Besa*," I said.

81

"*Baesa*," he repeated with a grimace, as if he could not get his tongue round the word, and could barely extract it from his mouth.

"For years on end, there were successive investigations to shed light on the secret. All kinds of suspicions were raised, and all kinds of explanations were given, but later all these were forgotten and it remained a legend."

"Thank God," he said. "It would be a sin to lose such a pearl."

My pleasure that he appreciated the legend so much led me to say things that I would otherwise kept to myself. I said, for instance, that whereas the Orthodox Church had several times tried to prohibit it, the ballad was now sung everywhere, even at the Easter celebrations, and not only at feasts in Arberia, but throughout all the territories of the Balkans.

He listened to me, all eyes and ears.

Because we fight over everything here on this peninsula, and not only over pastures and sheep, you can imagine that there have been quarrels even over the authorship of these legends.

"Just think of that," he said.

"Even though everybody insists on claiming this legend for themselves, our monks think that it was born here. This is not only because the event really happened in this country, but also because only among the Albanians has the *besa* become so charged with meaning.

"No doubt," he said. His eyes remained half-closed and it seemed that his mind was elsewhere. "Magnificent," he murmured. "The living and the dead trying to climb on the same cart . . . because, as we know, there is something dead in every living person, and vice versa."

He talked as if to himself, and meanwhile covered half his face with the collar of his cloak.

"I am keeping my left eye from the wind," he said to me, although I had not shown any sign of suspicion.

For part of the way, we spoke about other legends. They always concerned this failure to make the crossing, and an attempt to do so. A man who tried to climb out of the pit of hell. Another who, having been transformed into a snake, attempted again to assume human form. A wall, that demanded a sacrifice in order not to fall . . .

"A sacrifice?" he almost shrieked.

His brow darkened, but this was not gloom but the opening of a chasm. He continued to hide half his face with his collar, but even what was visible was enough to make your flesh creep.

"A wall demanding a sacrifice . . . This is the legend of immurement, if I am not mistaken."

"It is, sir," I replied, rather coldly, I do not know why. "But you seem to know it."

"I know it. But I would love to hear it again. Tell it to me," he said in a lost voice, as if to say "help."

He now seemed far away from me, despite his attempts to smile. I could almost sense the reason for his anxiety. It was somewhere close to me. I could almost touch it. Ah, give it a moment, I thought, give it a moment. It will appear of its own accord.

"A wall, that demanded a human being locked within it . . . as it were to acquire a soul . . . tell it to me," he said again. "And don't think the worse of me. I am a bit of a child, and when I like something, I like to hear it a dozen, a hundred times."

I began to tell him the legend of the castle of Shkodra,

just as I had heard it years ago from my mother. There were three brothers, all masons, who were building the walls, but their work was not going well, because what they built in the day was destroyed in the night.

Suddenly, the reason for his disquiet became as clear to me as daylight. You had to have the brains of Gjelosh not to grasp the similarity between the castle in the legend and their damaged bridge.

"What they built during the day was destroyed in the night," he murmured in a soporific voice, as if lulling himself to sleep.

I could not look him in the eye.

"What could they do?" I went on, involuntarily lowering my voice. "A wise old man told them that the wall collapsed because it demanded a sacrifice. And so they decided to immure one of their wives in the foundations.

"A sacrifice."

"Yes, a sacrifice," I whispered. "Since to immure someone means killing them."

"Killing them . . ."

"Of course. They say that even if a person's shadow is walled up inside a bridge, that person, so all the more reason . . ."

"Yes, yes," he groaned.

"But which wife?" I continued. "They argued over the matter at great length and decided to sacrifice the wife who brought them their midday meal the next day."

"But," he interrupted. "But . . ."

"They gave their *besa* to each other that they would not tell their wives about the decision they had made. And so, as you see, we have the *besa* again. Or rather the *besa* and treachery woven together."

"Yes, *baesa*."

The word now seemed to stretch and tear at the corners of his mouth, and I would not have been surprised to see a trickle of blood.

I wanted to say that here, just as in the first tale, the motif of the *besa*, according to our monks, proves the Albanian authorship of the ballad. But there was some kind of . . . how shall I put it? . . . fatal urgency in his expression that forced me too to speed up my tales.

"But that night two brothers, the oldest and the second, told their wives the secret and so broke the *besa*. The youngest brother kept it."

"Ah."

"The two older brothers broke the *besa*," I repeated, hardly able to swallow my saliva.

This was exactly the right place to explain to him that these words "to break the *besa*" are, in the Slavic version of the ballad, *vjeru pogazio*, which mean "to violate faith" or "to outrage religion", and are quite meaningless in the Slavic version. This is because of an erroneous translation from the Albanian, mistaking the word *besa* for *besim*, meaning belief, religion. However, he would not let me pause. He had grasped my hand, and softly, very softly, as if asking me about a secret, he said, "and then?"

"Then morning came, and when their mother-in-law as usual tried to send one of the wives with food for the masons, the two older wives who knew the secret pretended to be sick. So the youngest set out, and they immured her, and that is all."

I raised my eyes to look at his face, and almost cried out. All the moisture of his old man's eyes had drained away, and those empty eyes now resembled the cavities in a statue. Like death, I thought. That is how her eyes must have looked.

31

THROUGHOUT THE following days, he kept seeking me out, and as soon as he found me he would do what he could to bring the conversation round to the immurement of the bride. He spoke of it as if it were an event that had happened only two weeks before, as if he was charged with its investigation. Gradually, he involved me too. For hours on end, I could think of nothing but a semi-desert place under a scorching sun, where three masons kept building walls that could never be finished. As we talked about the legend, we carefully analysed it strand by strand, trying to account for its darker sides, and to find a pattern of logic amid its apparent contradictions.

He asked me which of the three wives had children, and whether perhaps the youngest had none, as was easy to believe, and whether this was the reason why she was the one who was sacrificed. But I explained to him that all three had children, and I even apologized for not telling him the end of the story, in which the young wife who was immured begged her murderers (I used the actual word) to leave one of her breasts outside the wall, so that even after her death she could suckle her child. He nearly lost his temper at my omission, shaking his finger almost threateningly at me, and told me not to do such a thing ever again. Because we were both of us at the time steeped in a strange world, his threat made no impression on me, although this is not something that I could normally forgive anyone. At this point, I also told him about the curse which the sacrificed wife lays on the stonework in the two famous lines:

O tremble, wall of stone,
As I tremble in this wall!

"This can be taken in a technical way," he butted in. "Because . . . at least bridges . . . every bridge is subject to vibration the whole time.

This interjection on his part made no particular impression on me, but when a little later he said that immuring a person in fact weakens a structure, I interrupted:

"Tell me, please, whether you are a collector of tales or a builder."

"Oh," he said. "I'm in no way a builder, but I've learned something about the subject from working alongside builders. In fact, all great building works resemble crimes, and vice versa, crimes resemble . . ." He laughed. "For me, there is no difference between the two. Whenever I find myself in front of columns I can clearly see blood spattering the marble, and the victim might replace a cathedral."

One day he knocked before dawn to tell me something he had thought of during the night. I was still sleepy and could barely take in what he said. Finally, I understood. He was saying that in his opinion the youngest brother too must have told his wife everything on that unforgettable night before the sacrifice.

"How is that possible?" I said. "How could a young woman then go to the masons knowing the fate that awaited her?"

"I knew you would say that," he said. "But I have thought of everything." He moved closer to me. "Listen to this. The youngest wife agreed to be sacrificed voluntarily, because her sisters-in-law and mother-in-law had made life hell for her."

"Hmm," I said. "Rather strange."

"There is nothing strange about it," he went on. "Between a daily hell and immurement, she chose the latter. Do you know what a quarrel among sisters-in-law means? Ah, but of course, you're a monk."

"But what about him?" I asked. "What do you think about his attitude?"

"Whose?"

"Her husband's."

"I have thought long and hard about that too. No doubt he knew that she suffered, but never imagined that matters could be so bad as to drive her to self-destruction. So, the next day, when he saw his own wife arrive carrying the basket of food, his blood must have frozen. What do you think?"

"I don't know what to say," I replied. "Perhaps you are right, but perhaps it wasn't like that at all."

I was in fact certain that it had not been like that. Now whenever he came to see me, he had some new explanation. Once he told me that the youngest brother had perhaps not told his wife the secret, not out of a desire to keep the *besa* with his brothers, but because he did not love his wife and had found a way to get rid of her. Another time, he suggested that perhaps the three brothers had colluded among themselves to kill the youngest wife, and the whole fiction that the walls demanded a sacrifice was just a way of justifying the murder. All his interpretations of the legend were founded on wickedness, betrayal, and disloyalty, and whenever he left I would be annoyed with myself for having listened to him. When he departed for the last time, he had sown the seed of doubt over the behaviour not only of the three mason brothers and the two sisters-in-law, but also that of the mother-in-law, who in his view certainly was party to the oath, and even the behaviour of the sacrificed wife herself. After he had left, after slinging mud at everything, not sparing even the dead, I decided I would tell him that he was free to think what he liked, but I had no desire to hear any more of his perverted speculations.

I waited for him the next day, to tell him that his efforts to throw mud at this old tragedy were useless, because the true kernel of the legend was the idea that all labour, and every major task, requires some kind of sacrifice, and that this magnificent idea is embodied in the mythologies of many peoples. What was new, and peculiar to the ballad of the Balkan peoples, was that the sacrifice was not connected with the outbreak of war or some march, nor even a religious rite, but concerned a wall, a work of construction. And this can perhaps be explained by the fact that the first inhabitants of these territories, the Pelasgians, were the first masons in the world, as the ancient Greek chronicles themselves admit.

I wanted to say that in truth the drops of blood in the legend were nothing but streams of sweat, but we know that sweat is a kind of humble nameless servant in comparison with blood, and therefore nobody has devoted songs and ballads to it. So it can be considered normal in a song to represent a river of sweat with a few drops of blood. It is of course obvious that alongside his sweat every man sacrifices something of himself, like the youngest brother, who sacrificed his own happiness.

I could hardly wait to impart to him these and other ideas of mine, but just when I had made up my mind to speak out, he disappeared. I never saw him again.

32

I N SPITE of the severe cold, work on the bridge continued.
It was said that they had now quite completed the second
main arch and had begun the third. I say "it was said," because
in fact nothing could be discerned from the bridge's external
appearance, behind its confusion of timbers!

Nothing worth recording occurred in the following
weeks. The old blackened raft continued to pass from one
bank to the other. The ferryman looked more hunchbacked
than ever. The words "Ferries and Rafts" on the rusty sign
were barely legible, while two planks of the raft broke loose,
and no one bothered to repair them. Everything now
quickly decayed, and the black water visible through the
gaping planks of the raft seemed to make the expressions of
its passengers even gloomier.

At dusk one Sunday (this is the only event that I can even
partially remember), some people wearing black sheepskins
crossed the river by raft, in sombre haste. The fog seemed
to swallow them as soon as they disembarked on the opposite bank. It was not long before some more people, also in
black sheepskins, asked for the ferry. They were just as
gloomy and in as great a hurry as the first group. They asked
about the men who had crossed before, and these were the
only words to escape their lips as they crossed the river. One
of them vomited continuously.

33

ONE MORNING, as I walked along the frozen riverbank in the hope of catching sight of the collector of
tales and legends (for I did not know then that he had
vanished for ever), I came face to face with the foreman.
The north wind was piercing. It had frozen his eyes in
particular, coating them with a kind of glittering film that
prevented you from seeing what was inside them.

To my astonishment, this stern, taciturn man greeted me.
Only then did I realize how eager I was to get to know him.
We exchanged a few words and set off walking side by side
along the riverbank. The icy crust that coated his eyes
seemed to have cracked in two or three places, making them
even more inscrutable. I had imagined that talking with this
man would be difficult, but not to this extent. Our conversation was a rambling, muddled affair, a real maze from
which you could not extricate yourself. It was evident that
he himself found it painful. It was apparently easier for him
to construct bridges or towers than an ordinary man-to-
man conversation. The worst of it was that I still sensed that
something valuable, perhaps extremely valuable, lay at the
bottom of this tangle, and it was precisely my efforts to
understand this that upset me most. When I left him I felt
as if my head was cleft in two. I sat down by the fire and
once more did my best to make some sense out of the

tangle. I began to unravel it carefully, thread by thread, and eventually I seemed to succeed. The essence of what he had said was this: according to signs that he had been studying for some time, the lineaments of a new order that would carry the world many centuries forward had faintly, ever so faintly, begun to appear in this part of Europe. These signs included the opening of new banks in Durrës, growing numbers of Jewish and Italian money-lenders dealing in twenty-seven different kinds of currency, and the almost universal acceptance of the Venetian ducat as a form of international tender. There was also the increasingly heavy traffic of merchant caravans, the organization of trade fairs and especially (Oh, Lord! How he emphasized that word "especially"), especially the construction of roads and bridges in stone. And all this movement, he said, was simultaneously a sign of life and death, of the birth of a new world and the death of the old. He talked about bridges and the difficulties of building them, and during this part of the conversation I felt as if I were crushed under the rubble of a bridge that he had brought down on top of me. But then he explained to me that, of all the monstrosities that deface the earth's surface, there never had been and never would be anything uglier than corpse-bridges. These bridges are stillborn, he said, and they live in death (he used the phrase, "their life is a prolonged dying" until the time comes for their demolition (or "ultimate death" as he put it). He told me that he had built such bridges himself and that now they appeared in his dreams like ghosts. If ever he decided to commit suicide (he told me), he would hang himself from such a bridge. I could scarcely understand what they were. They were not bridges built over rivers or streams or chasms, or indeed over any kind of gap that had to be crossed. They were bridges built in the middle of fields, and their only service was now and then to carry on their backs great ladies, who climbed on them in order to observe the sunset together with their guests. Building bridges was in fashion now, he said, and many princes and pashas considered them to be the same as the porches of their houses. I have built such phantoms, he said. He indicated with his hand the furrowed, foaming waters of the Ujana e Keqe over which the stone bridge loomed, grim and unloved, and he added: "But this kind of bridge, even if washed in blood, is a thousand times more useful than those."

And that was more or less my conversation with him.

34

IN THE first week of March the bridge was damaged again. This time, the damage was entirely below the waterline, and was extremely worrying. Large stone blocks had been dislodged from the piers of the main arch, and this, they said, would endanger the whole central portion of the bridge if repairs were not made at once.

Suspended by ropes above the icy water, the workmen attempted to fill the cavities. Besides being an exceptionally difficult task, this patchwork seemed in vain as long as the stones were put in place without mortar. However, if the repairs were postponed until summer, when the waters subsided and the use of mortar became possible, there was a danger that the waters would further erode the cavities.

Like so many idlers bent over a victim's wounds, new faces kept appearing as the news got about, and people came swarming all day over the damage. It was said that a new way of fixing stones was to be tried with a mixture of wool, pitch, and egg-white.

The new damage to the bridge caused, as expected, a fresh storm of evil premonitions. People came from all over to see it with their own eyes, the cursed bridge which had brought down on itself the wrath of the naiads and water-spirits. That the damage was invisible made it all the more frightening.

Together with the curious travellers, a horde of bards came, some returning in disappointment from an unfinished war somewhere among the principalities of the north, and others appearing here for the first time. These latter took their places at the Inn of the Two Roberts, and every night sang old ballads in eerie voices.

They told me that one of these ballads was that of the three mason brothers and the young wife immured in the castle that was built by day and destroyed at night. I remembered the collector of tales and myths, but I do not know what it was that impelled me to set off for the Inn of the Two Roberts to listen to the ballad with my own ears.

It was chilly, but nevertheless I set off on foot. Perhaps because of the potholes and puddles on the highway, I could not banish from my mind the watery eyes of the vanished collector of tales.

As soon as I heard the ballad's first verses, I recognized his hand in its composition. The ballad had been changed. It was not about three brothers building a castle wall, but about dozens of masons building a bridge. The bridge was built during the day and destroyed at night by the spirits of the water. It demanded a sacrifice. Let someone come who is willing to be sacrificed in the piers of the bridge, the bards sang. Let him be a sacrifice for the sake of the thousands and thousands of travellers who will cross this bridge winter and summer, in rain and storm, journeying towards their joy or to their misfortune, hordes of people down the centuries to come.

"Have you heard this new ballad that has appeared?" the innkeeper said to me. "The old one was better."

I did not know what to say. The bard sang on in a spine-chilling voice:

O tremble, bridge of stone
As I tremble in this wall.

"Yesterday I heard them say that every bridge does in fact tremble a little, all the time," the innkeeper went on.

I nodded. There flashed through my mind the thought that the collector of tales knew something about bridge-building, perhaps as much as the foreman.

I returned homeward in utter misery. From a distance, the bridge stood blue in the falling dusk. Even if it were washed a thousand times in blood . . . the foreman had said.

Clearly the ballad portended nothing but blood.

All the way back, all I could think of was the coming sacrifice. My head swam. Would he come to the bridge himself, like the youngest brother's wife, or would he be caught in a trap? Who would it be? What reason would he have to die, or to be killed? The old ballad entangled itself in my head with the new one, like two trees unsuccessfully trying to graft themselves onto each other. What would happen the evening before in the house of the man to be sacrificed? And what would be his reason for setting out to die, on a moonless night, as the old song put it.

Nobody will come, I suddenly said almost aloud. That collector of tales was just mad. But deep in my heart I felt afraid that someone would come. He would come slowly, with soft footsteps through the darkness, and lay his head on the sacrificial block. "Who are you who will come?" I asked myself. "And why will you come?"

35

SOME TRAVELLERS who stopped at the Inn of the Two Roberts brought disturbing news. The Turks had finally succeeded in forcing Byzantium to cede its part, in other words half, of the Vlora base in a few months' time. What they had sought from Aranit Komneni for so long in vain, they had managed to snatch from the ailing empire. If this grim news was indeed true, Aranit Komneni would from now on share the base as a "partner" with the royal Turkish tiger. And it is well known what life is like when one is caged with a tiger.

The news shocked everybody, especially our liege lord. People said that Aranit had sent letters to all the Albanian nobles and that a state of war had all but been declared in Vlora.

36

T HE MARCH days rolled by like so many icicles. Nobody could remember such a bitterly cold spring in years. The news about the Orikum base at Vlora was true. The decision to hand over the Byzantine portion of the base to the Turkish Empire was proclaimed by special decree in the two imperial capitals, Constantinople and Brusa.

The news caused deep despair everywhere. It passed the comprehension of the European courts, it was said, that age-old Byzantium could submit to such an indignity. Some made allowances, saying that this was at present the only way of staving off the Turkish monster. At present . . . But later?

News came from Vlora of preparations for the evacuation of the Byzantine warships. Apparently the base would be vacated very soon. The Scandinavian garrison too was preparing to make way for the Turks. The elderly prince of Vlora kept his army mobilized. They said that he himself was seriously ill, but was keeping his illness secret.

As if these dark clouds were not enough, the bards at the Inn of the Two Roberts continued singing about the sacrifice that must be made at the bridge.

Work proceeded feverishly on the bridge. Ever since I had heard the most recent ballad, in which the immured victim cursed the bridge to perpetual trembling, it seemed to me that the bridge had really begun to shake.

37

FOR SEVERAL consecutive days, carts loaded with barrels of pitch passed along the western highway. The ferryman poled them across the river, cursing the wagoners, the pitch, and the world at large.

They said that the pitch was urgently needed at the Vlora base. That is how it has always happened. As soon as tar begins to move fast along the highways, you know that blood will flow after it.

Meanwhile, dire foreboding continually thickened around us, or, I would say, around everything that centred upon this cursed bridge. Now it was not merely the bards who went on casting their grim spell night and day at the Inn of the Two Roberts. No, this matter was now a topic of general conversation from morning to night; strangest of all, it became a most simple and natural thing to talk about a sacrifice, as if it were about the weather or the crops. The idea of sacrifice, up to now a truth within a ballad, had emerged from its cocoon and had suddenly crept up on us. Now it moved among us, alive, and on equal terms with all the other concerns of the day.

On the roads, at home, and in taverns along the great highway, people talked of the reward the bridge and road builders would give to the family of the man who would allow himself to be sacrificed in the bridge piers. I could not accustom myself to this transition at all. Things that had been savage and frightening until yesterday had suddenly become tame. Everybody talked about the sum of money the immured man's family would receive, and people even said that, apart from the cash payment, they would receive for a long time to come a percentage of the profits from the bridge, like everyone else who had met its expenses. Other people had even stranger details to relate. They said that the compensation due to every member of the family had been worked out in the minutest detail, with every kind of eventuality borne in mind. Everything had been provided for, from the possibility of the victim being without relatives, an odd-man-out, as they say (which was difficult to believe), to the opposite case of a poor man who might have a wife, parents, and a dozen children. They had anticipated everything, from the possibility of a man without issue (in which case, in the absence of heirs, the remaining portion of the reward would be spent on a chapel for his soul to be built just next to the bridge piers), to the case of a needy man, who would be given a first and final chance of property to leave to his nearest and dearest, in just the same way as a meadow or a mill is left as a bequest, except that this property would be his death. They said that the planning had been so thorough that they had even provided for the sacrifice of rich men, in other words death for a whim, out of boredom with life, or simply for the sake of fame. In this case, if the immured victim did not care for the reward, the cash would be used to erect, besides the chapel, a statue or memorial, always next to the bridge piers.

They said that all these calculations had been put down on paper and fixed with a seal, so that anybody who was thinking of being immured could read them beforehand.

To me all this resembled a bizarre dream. This was something we had never heard of before, a kind of death with accounts, seals, and percentages. We were quite unused to it. Sometimes I could not take it in at all. I called to mind the delegation and its talks with the count, and what the collector of legends and the bridge's foreman had said, and I tried to establish some connection between these things, but the more I brooded the more perplexed I became. This business of a tariff for the sacrifice left me quite confused.

Sometimes I told myself that perhaps these were the signs of the new order which the foreman had told me about in that unforgettable conversation. That jumble of words had been full of contracts, accounts, currency exchange, and percentages, percentages, percentages on everything. Even on death.

38

I<small>T WEIGHED</small> on me like a fatal burden. Its stone piers crushed me. One of its arches planted itself directly on my stomach, another on my throat. I wanted to break free and save myself from it, but it was impossible. The only movement I could make was a slight, a very slight tremor . . . Ah yes, I thought, this was the perpetual trembling of which the ballad spoke. A cry rose in my throat. The cry struggled to come out, pressing against the stone arch. This went on a long time. Then, I do not know how, something was released inside me, and I budged. In that same moment, with eyes closed in terror, I felt the bridge collapse and fall on my body.

I woke drenched in sweat. The room was stuffy. I rose to open the window. Outside, a warm, damp wind blew. One could sense that the sky, though invisible, was overcast. Some silent flashes of lightning burst against the mute flatness.

"Oh Lord," I cried aloud, and I lay down again on my bed. But further sleep eluded me. A few awkward ideas, with a deceptive glitter as if frozen by winter, floated somewhere inside me. I do not know how long I remained in this state. When I finally opened my eyes, it was light. Somebody was knocking at the outside door. There was an anxious rattle at the iron doorlatch. The sky was cloudy, but not as overcast as I had imagined. Spring comes without warning, the sap rises, I said to myself.

Two village neighbours were at the door, with distraught faces. There was dismay in their bloodshot eyes.

"What is it?" I asked. "What's the matter?"

They raised their hands to their throats, as if trying to force out the words.

"At the bridge, Gjon . . . Under the first arch . . . They've walled up Murrash Zenebisha."

"No!"

I was unable to say anything else, or even think. But these people, who seemed to have lost the power of thought before me, expected something from me. Soon I found myself walking towards the bridge. We hardly walked, but were blown where the wind bore us, like three waving scraps of rag, myself in the middle, and the others on either side.

I knew Murrash Zenebisha. Among ordinary people, it would have been difficult to find anyone more common-place than him. His appearance, his average height, and his whole life were ordinary to the point of weariness. I could not take in the fact that this extraordinary thing, immure-ment, had happened to none other than him. The more I thought about it the more it seemed an aberration. It was more than turning into a leader or a statue . . . Everything had gone too far . . . now he was divided from us by the mortar of legend.

From a distance, you could see a small gathering of people round the bridge pier. By the first arch. He must be there.

As I drew closer, I tried, I do not know why, to recall Murrash Zenebisha's unremarkable face. Oh Lord, from this moment I could not picture it in my mind at all. It swam as if under a film of water, with a broken, uncanny smile.

The small group moved silently to make room for me. Nobody greeted me. They stood like candles, looking strangely small against the background of the bridge. A part of the arch bent heavy and chill above them.

"There he is," a quiet voice said to me.

He was there, white like a mask, spattered with lime, only his head and neck, and part of his chest. The remainder of his trunk and his arms and legs were merged with the wall.

I could not tear my eyes from him. There were traces of fresh mortar everywhere. The wall had been strengthened to contain the sacrifice. (A body walled up in the piers of a bridge weakens the structure, the collector of legends had said.) The bulging wall looked as if it were pregnant. Worse, it looked as if it were in birthpangs.

The body seemed planted in the stone. His stomach and legs and the main portion of his trunk were rooted deep, and only a small portion of him emerged.

A wall that demands a human being in its cavity, the collector of of legends had said. Foul, sinful visions taunted me. The wall indeed looked pregnant . . . But this was a perverse pregnancy . . . No baby emerged from it, on the contrary, a human being was swallowed up . . . It was worse than perverse. It would have been perverse if, in contrast to a baby who emerges to the light, the man who entered the darkness were to shrink and be reduced to the size of an infant and then to nothing . . . But that was not to happen. This was a perversion of everything. It was perversity itself.

Around me, people's voices came as if from the next world.

"When?" asked the hushed voice of a new arrival.

"Just after midnight."

"Did he feel much pain?"

"None at all."

I heard sobbing close beside me. Then I saw his wife. Her face was swollen with tears and in her arms she carried a year-old baby, who was trying to nuzzle her breast. Paying no attention to the men standing around, she had uncovered one breast. The breast was swollen with milk and the nipple occasionally escaped from the baby's mouth. Her tears fell on her large white breast and when the nipple missed the child's mouth, her tears mixed with drops of milk.

"He was very calm," explained one of the count's scribes, who had apparently come in search of explanations. "He asked about the terms of the agreement one more time and then . . ."

A mason who stood holding a pail near the place of sacrifice splashed the dead man with wetlime. The liquid trickled down the hair sticking to his brow, gave a sudden gleam to his open eyes, which was quickly quenched, and then patchily smeared his features before coursing down his neck and disappearing into the wall.

"Why are you throwing on whitewash?" a nervous voice asked. But no one replied.

It seemed that they were sprinkling him at intervals, because after emptying its contents over the victim, the mason went to refill his bucket from a nearby barrel.

His wife's interrupted sobbing became louder after the sprinkling.

"He didn't tell anyone about what he was going to do?" someone asked his wife softly.

She shook her head.

"No one," she said.

Only then I noticed the other members of the family, standing round his wife. His parents and two brothers with their wives were there. Their faces were petrified, as if they too had been splashed with that lime of eternity.

"No one," his wife repeated. But I could not look at her eyes any longer, they were so swollen with weeping.

The count's scribe asked something of her too, and she gave a short answer. Then he turned to me and said something, but my eyes were fixed on the immured man; I stared at the lower part of his neck, at his collar-bone, just where the cavity above his chest . . .

But at that moment, the man standing by with the pail of whitewash in his hands splashed him again, and once more the liquid ran down the forehead, igniting and at once quenching his vacant, blind, oblivious white eyes. Then the trickle meandered down his neck, quickly whitening the very spot from which I could not tear my eyes.

The baby had again missed his mother's nipple, and was whimpering. I asked the woman whether they had been in financial straits.

"No," she said. "He'd been earning plenty recently."

Recently, I thought. Like many inhabitants of the surrounding district, he had been working as a day labourer on the bridge and must have been receiving a normal wage, as normal as everything else in his life.

Another of the count's men arrived and whispered the same questions.

"When?"

"Just after midnight."

It seemed that we would all stand rooted to the spot, and people would arrive and mutter the same questions until the end of time.

Now and again one could hear the words "brother, brother" from his sister. But his mother's sobbing was more muffled. Only once, she said, "They've killed you, my son." And a little later, she very softly added, "As if your mother had no need of you."

I would never have dared to interrupt a mother's lament, but the words "They've killed you, my son" gave me no peace.

"Is it possible they've killed him?" I said to her in a low voice. "But why?"

She wiped her tears.

"Why? How should a poor old woman like me know? No doubt for nothing. Because he cast a shadow on this earth."

"He had been very low these last days," said his wife by my shoulder. "He had something on his mind."

"And last night?"

"Last night particularly."

My eyes froze again on the dead man's neck just above the collar-bone, as if something were about to appear there, a shadow, a . . . I do not know what to say. But the mason with his usual gesture once more emptied his pail of whitewash over the immured man. The greyish-white liquid, the very stuff of legend, poured over him.

"Last night particularly," his wife went on. "At midnight he seemed to be moving and getting up. At dawn he was gone."

The milk from her breast had again missed her baby and trickled to the ground, but she seemed not to care.

"Did you need money?" someone asked.

"What can I say?" his wife asked. "Like everyone else."

The members of the dead man's family still stood grouped in silence. There was the splashing of the pail again as it was refilled with whitewash from the barrel. I was completely numbed. I would not have been surprised if the man with the bucket had now coated us all with lime.

39

ALL THAT day and the next, I remained obsessed with the sight I had seen. His open eyes congealed under their film of whitewash seemed to stare from every wall around me. Walls terrified me, and I tried at all costs not to look at them. But they were almost impossible to avoid. I only then understood what an important and powerful part walls play in our lives. Like conscience, there is no getting away from them. I could leave the parish house, but even outside there were walls, close by or in the distance.

My head was splitting in two with speculation. If he had really set out to sacrifice himself of his own free will, as everybody now claimed, what must his motive have been? The desire to ensure a better life for his wife and family, with the help of the great sum of money that the construction company would pay for the sacrifice? I could have believed this of many people but not of the unassuming Murrash Zenebisha. Sometimes I wondered whether he had gone to die in order to escape a family quarrel (the sheer hell of sisters-in-law living under one roof is beyond imagining), but this too was scarcely likely. There had never been the least rumour of such a thing in the Zenebisha family. I sometimes asked myself whether, whatever his reasons for sacrificing himself, he had told his wife what he was planning. And if so, had she approved of it? That was beyond belief. And then I wondered whether he perhaps did not love his wife. She had said that he sometimes went away at night, she did not know where. She had even begun to grow suspicious.

I knew myself that this was the kind of conjecture which, although I despised it, I had nevertheless acquired from that collector of customs. I strove to free myself from it, as from the walls, but I was obsessed with the idea.

Sometimes he would go out at night . . . Was his wife really telling the truth? Were the others telling the truth? I too could have believed what was said, but that place in the victim's neck, there between his neck and collar-bone, put everything in question. I had stared at it three times, because each time it had struck me that a spot under the layer of whitewash had begun to blush faintly, very faintly, like a stain. But all three times the man with the pail had splashed liquid on the victim before I could really detect any redness.

Enough, I thought. We have had nothing but babble and lies. We were dealing with a crime pure and simple. Murrash Zenebisha had been murdered. His mother had been the first to say the word: "They murdered him for nothing . . . Because he cast a shadow on this earth . . ." They had murdered him in cold blood shortly after midnight and then walled him up. The wound, or one of his wounds, was between the neck and the collar-bone, and the man with the pail had splashed whitewash over him again and again to hide the possible bloodstain. It was a murder done by the road builders.

But how had Murrash Zenebisha come to be by the bridge at night? I asked this question out loud, because I had the satisfaction of being able to supply a clear answer.

111

Sometimes he would go out at night . . . And so shall we do the murder ourselves? . . . The road builders had let slip these words at the meeting with the count. Murrash Zenebisha's fate had been sealed on that day. And the count, refusing to have anything to do with this murky business, washed his hands like Pontius Pilate. Murrash Zenebisha's fate had no doubt been sealed at that moment. The road builders had discovered that the water people were paying someone to damage the bridge at night. This person was none other than the unassuming Murrash Zenebisha. He had done his job three times without getting caught. The fourth time they had caught him in the act and killed him. He had been very low recently. He had something on his mind . . . And last night? Last night particularly. He must have felt the net closing on him. Everywhere bards were singing of his death. His only way out was to give up this work of destruction. However "Ferries and Rafts" were not ready to see the agreement broken. After catching him in their trap, they would not let him back out. So there was nothing for him to do but to become an outlaw, or to continue on his fatal path. Apparently he had chosen the second option. So he had something on his mind. And last night? Last night particularly. Possibly this was to have been his last assignment for the water people. He set out as on the other occasions shortly after midnight. He dived into the water a long way from the bridge and swam up to it, trying not to make any noise. The night was dark, there was no moon. What happened next at the bridge, no one would ever know. Perhaps they caught him on the spot, dislodging the stones, or in the water, trying to escape; no one knew. No one knew how they had killed him. They may have killed him at once, or perhaps they interrogated him for a time, and threatened him. Or they may have talked to him sweetly and reassuringly, reminding him of the lavish compensation his wife would receive. Or perhaps there had been neither threats nor inducements, and they killed him in silence, and everything was done without words, in dumb show, under the arch of the bridge. Because this was only the final act of a murder which had been in the wind for a long time. Its spurts of blood had already spattered us all, and its screams had died away long ago.

The long duel between the men of the water and the men of the land had concluded with the victory of the latter. Do not try to harm us again, or you will be killed. That was the cry that came from the first arch of the bridge.

I was convinced of the truth of all this. But my mind was not entirely settled, and I continued silently to mull over innumerable theories.

If this was really what had happened, then the question followed of whether Murrash Zenebisha's wife was aware that he had agreed with "Ferries and Rafts" to damage the bridge. And, if she did know, what had been her attitude? But the initial question cropped up again before this. What had led Murrash Zenebisha into this pact with "Ferries and Rafts"? Money? He was earning well enough. Besides, his brothers were masons like himself and earned as much as he did.

All this made my head swim. I felt that I had wandered into a maze of arguments from which I would never emerge. I returned to where I had started and circled around the same point: had his wife encouraged him in this affair or, on the contrary, held him back? Neither was to be ruled out. Perhaps she had dreamed of a better life, of dressing better than her sisters-in-law, of finery. But it was also possible that she had said to her husband: what do we need this damned money for? Thank God, we don't live too badly. Sometimes he would go out at night . . . And she had even several times become suspicious. But what if he really wanted more money for another woman? He would go out at night . . . There could be two reasons for his disappearing at night. Either to damage the bridge, or to meet another woman. Or perhaps both together. Another woman, rather than the vicissitudes of his daily round, was more likely to lead him to risk his life. His wife had become suspicious. Perhaps she had spied on him. He could have explained his absences by telling her about damaging the bridge (if he had indeed told her his secret). But even so, perhaps his wife had begun not to trust him. So she might have followed him on one of those nights, and when she discovered that he had a secret besides the bridge, she may in her subsequent fury (or who knows, quite calmly) have informed the builders.

But in whatever way the incident had happened, its essence remained unchanged: the bridge builders had murdered Murrash Zenebisha in cold blood and walled him up. The crime had only one purpose – to inspire terror.

They had calculated everything in advance. No doubt they had carried out detailed studies of all possible ways of justifying the crime. At the very beginning, before the bridge existed even as a plan, they had started by sending a man who pretended to be seized by an epileptic fit on the very bank of the Ujana e Keqe. Not a bridge, not a sketch, but a sickness lay at the root of it all. That was the first blow. It was natural that death should follow.

Both sides, "Ferries and Rafts" and the construction company, used the ancient legend in their savage contest.

The former used the legend to spread the idea of destroying the bridge, and the latter used the legend to plot a murder.

My exhausted brain contained an idea that was as dismal as it was wearyingly plain. I thought that, like all the affairs of this world, this story was both simpler and more involved than it appeared . . . They had come from far away. One side came from the water, and the other from the steppes, in order to accomplish before our eyes something that, as their collector of customs said, could still not be understood for what it was: the building of a bridge or a crime. For it was still unknown which of the two would survive longer on this earth and which would be eroded by the seasons. Only then would we understand which was the real edifice and which the mere scaffolding that helped in its construction, the pretext that justified it.

At first sight, it seemed that the newcomers had calculated everything, but perhaps that too was only a superficial view of things. Perhaps they themselves imagined they were building a bridge, but in fact, as if in delirium, they had obeyed another order, whose origin they themselves did not understand. And all of us, under the same illusion, watched it and were unable to discern what lay before our eyes: stone arches, whitewash, or blood.

Holy Mary, forgive us our sins, I silently prayed. I succeeded in calming my soul, but my brain would not rest. It raced to the legend. These people had revived a legend like an old weapon discovered accidentally to give each other savage wounds. It was nevertheless early to say whether they had really enlisted it in their service. Perhaps it was the legend itself that had caught them in a snare, had clouded their minds, and had instigated the bloody game.

40

URING ALL those days, nobody talked of anything but the immurement of Murrash Zenebisha. People told the most incredible stories about what he supposedly said at the moment when they walled him in, and his last wish for a space to be left for his eyes so that he could see his year-old child. Some substituted the bridge itself for the child, and some tied his last wish not only to his family but to his sense of duty, to the spirits, to the entire principality.

There was a constant little crowd of people on the sand-bank by the arch of the bridge where the victim was immured. The guards placed by the count watched over the body from morning to night, while the investigator assigned to probe the incident would hover about and sooner or later come and plant himself in front of the victim. His face, that chalky white mask, had undergone no change since the first day. Now that the whitewash was dry and they were no longer coating him, the whiteness of that face was never changed. They said that if you looked at it by moonlight, you could be struck dumb.

His family, his elderly parents, his brothers and their wives, and his young widow with her baby, whose mother's nipple always missed his mouth, came every day and stood stock still for hours on end, never taking their eyes off the victim. His open eyes encrusted in whitewash had the mute unresponsiveness of that "irreversibility" that only death can bring. That first week, his parents aged by a century, and the features of his brothers and their wives and even their infants seemed furrowed for life. While he, leaning against the arch of the bridge as if against a stone pillar, entirely smoothed over, studied them from beyond the chalky barrier that made him more remote than a spirit.

Whenever the crowd thinned or dispersed, mad Gjelosh the idiot would arrive at the site of the sacrifice. He was quite stunned by the scene, and his inability to understand what had happened mortified him considerably. He would walk slowly up to the body, approaching it sidelong, and softly whisper, "Murrash, Murrash," in the hope of making the man hear. He would repeat this many times and then disconsolately depart.

Old Ajkuna came on the seventh day, the day when it is believed that the dead make their first and most desperate attempt to break free of the shackles of the next world. She stayed for hours on end by the first arch, without uttering a word. Here was something which could find no parallel in the experience of even the most elderly. A few more days passed, and then whole weeks, and the fortieth day was approaching, the day on which it was believed that a dead man's eyeballs burst, and then everybody realized what a great burden an unburied man was, not only on his family, but on the entire district. It was something that violated everything we knew about the borders between life and death. The man remained poised between the two, like a bridge, without moving in one direction or the other. This man had sunk into nonexistence, but leaving his shape behind him above, like a forgotten garment.

People came from all parts to see the unburied body.

The curious came from distant villages, and wayfarers who lodged at the inns on the great highway; even rich foreigners came, as they travelled at their leisure to see the world together with their ladies. (Such a thing had come into fashion recently, after the dramatic improvements to the highway.)

They stood in awe by the first arch, noisy, waxen-faced, talking in their own languages and gesticulating. You could not tell from their gestures whether they blessed or cursed the hour that brought them to the bridge. Beyond all their hubbub, solitary, cold, vacant, aloof, and covered with lime, Murrash Zenebisha seemed to stand in silence like a veiled bride.

It was the beginning of April. The weather was fine and work proceeded on the bridge more busily than ever before. The dead man seemed to spur the work forward. The second span was now completely finished, and the vault of the third was being raised. Last year's filthy mud, which had dirtied everything round about, had gone. Now only a fine dust of noble whiteness fell from the carved stones and spread in all directions. It coated the two banks of the Ujana and sometimes on nights of full moon it shone and glittered in the distance.

On one of these moonlit April nights, I ran into the foreman on the riverbank, quite by accident. I had not seen him for a long time. He seemed not to want to look me in the eye. The words we exchanged were quite meaning-less and empty, like feathers that float randomly, lacking weight and reason. As we talked in our desultory way, I felt a sudden crazy urge to seize him by the collar of his cape, pin him against the bridge pier, and shout in his face: "That new world you told me about the other day, that new order with its banks and percentages, which is going to carry the world a thousand years forward, it too is soaked in blood."

I mentally said all this to him, and even expected his reply: "Yes, monk, like every kind of order." Meanwhile, as if he had sensed my inner turmoil, he raised his head and for the first time looked me in the eye. They were the same eyes that I now knew well, with rays and cracks, but inflamed, as if about to burst, almost as if the fortieth day had arrived not for the dead man at the bridge but for the foreman himself . . .

41

SPRING WAS exceptionally clear. The Ujana e Keqe brimmed with melted snow. Though full and reinvigorated, the river mounted no attack on the bridge. It seemed not to notice it any more. It foamed and seethed around the stone piers, under the feet of the dead, but as it flowed on it spread out again, as if pacified by the sight of the victim. Only in the cold crests of the waves a wicked, mocking glint remained.

All spring and at the beginning of summer, work continued unflaggingly. The third arch was almost finished, and work began on the relief arch of the right-hand approach.

Throughout its length, the bridge echoed to the sounds of masons' hammers, chisels, picks, and the creaking of the carts. Amidst the constant din of the building work and the roaring of the river, Murrash Zenebisha stood, coated as ever with whitewash, solitary, pallid, and alien. Whether the flesh of his face had decayed under his mask of lime, or whether it had hardened like mortar, nobody could tell.

His family came as always, but gradually reduced the length of their visits. Some days after his immurement, stunned by everything that had happened, they remembered that they had not even managed to weep for him according to custom. They tried to do so later, but it was impossible. Their laments stuck in their throats and the words that should have accompanied their weeping somehow would not come. Then they tried hiring professional mourners, but these women too, although practised in weeping under all kinds of circumstances, could not mourn, try as they might. He does not want to be wept for, his parents concluded.

It was now some while since his death, and at times it seemed a blessing to his family to have his living form in front of their eyes, but sometimes this seemed the worst curse of all. Now they no longer came together to visit him. His wife would come alone with her baby in her arms and, when she saw the others approaching, would step away. People said that there was a quarrel quietly brewing over the share of the compensation.

The investigators also came less frequently. It seems that the count had other preoccupations and would have liked to close the inquiry. However, this did not prevent the fame of Murrash Zenebisha from spreading further every day. It was said that he had become the conversational topic of the day in the large towns, and that the grand ladies of Durrës asked each other about him, as about the other novelties of the season.

Many people set off from distant parts with the sole object of seeing him. Sometimes they came with their wives, or even made the journey a second time. This was no doubt why the Inn of the Two Roberts had recently doubled its takings.

42

THE WEATHER deteriorated. The count, together with
his family, returned from the mountain lodge where he
had spent the summer. Night and day the din of hammers
was to be heard around the bridge. The work was nearing
its end. The left-hand approach arch was being finished.

One day at the beginning of September, the count's
daughter came to see the immured victim. I had not seen
her for some time. She had grown, and was now a fine
young woman. I feared she would not be able to bear the
sight of the dead man, but she endured it. As she left
the sandbank, thin, and somewhat woebegone, people
turned their heads after her. They knew that the powerful
Turkish pasha, whom ill fortune had recently made our
neighbour, had quarrelled with our liege lord because of
this dainty girl.

Perhaps because she had spent her girlhood in such
troubled times as recent seasons had been, no tales had been
woven round her, such as those about knights crossing seven
mountain ranges to meet a girl in secret, and the like,
such as are usually told about young countesses and the
daughters of nobles in general. In place of such tales of love,
there was only an alarming sobriquet attached to her, that,
I do not know why, spread everywhere. They called her
"the Turk's bride". I often racked my brains to explain such

an irrational nickname. It was quite meaningless. There was nothing to justify it because nothing like that had happened. It was the opposite of the truth, but the nickname clung to her. It could not conceivably have been created out of goodwill, or even out of malice, and so perhaps resembled a truth and a lie at the same time. The girl did not go to the Turks as a bride, but the nickname remained, as if it were unimportant whether the wedding took place or not, and the main thing was the proposal, and not its acceptance. And so she was called "the Turk's bride" simply because the Turks had asked for her, had cast their eyes this far, and had brandished from a distance that black veil with which they cover their women's faces.

The nickname made my flesh creep. Why was it still used, and why did it not perish the moment the Turks' proposal was rejected? What was this perpetual danger, this offer of marriage, that still floated on the wind? Sometimes I told myself that it was a chance nickname, more ridiculous than alarming, and nothing to become upset about, but it was not long before my suspicions were aroused again. Did it all not extend beyond the fate of the noble young lady? Did popular imagination in some obscure, utterly vague way perhaps foresee that this was to be the destiny for all the girls of Arberia? This horrible nickname could not have arisen for nothing, still less have stuck to her like a burr.

I said these things to myself, and thought: If only that young girl knew what I was thinking as she walks along the bank with her nurse, her slight figure almost translucent!

43

HASTE WAS evident everywhere: in the works on the Ujana, in the pace of the heralds, and even in the flight of the storks, which, having pecked at the beams of the bridge for one last time, set off on their distant migrations that no rivers or bridges could obstruct.

Even the news coming from the Orikum base was gathered in haste and was contradictory. It was said that the aged Komneni was dead, but that his death was being kept secret because of the situation at Orikum. All kinds of other things were whispered. It was said that the great Turkish sultan had withdrawn into the interior of Asia to meditate in complete solitude about the general affairs of the world, and that this was the reason why the Turks seemed to have fallen asleep.

There was no sign of them. But one day, at the end of the week, another dervish was seen, wandering across the cold plain, a solitary wind-whipped figure. Like all itinerant dervishes, he was barefoot and dust-covered, and perhaps for this reason seemed to have ash-coloured rags instead of hair, and hair instead of rags. He paused at the first arch of the bridge, fell on his face in front of the victim, and intoned an Islamic prayer in a deep and mournful voice. Then he disappeared again, I know not where, across the open plain.

44

A FEW days before the final work on the bridge, one of the foreman's two assistants, the fat one, fell ill with a rare and frightening disease: all the hairs on his body fell out. They shut him in a hut and tried in every possible way to keep his sickness secret, but there was no way it could be concealed. People gossiped about it all day, some with pity, some with fear, but most with mockery. Wolves moult in summer, they said, just like that. Gjelosh the idiot wandered all day round the hut, putting his eye to cracks in the wall to see what he could. Then he emerged from the other side, nodding his head as if in understanding. Old Ajkuna said that this was only the beginning of God's punishment. Everybody who had taken part in this cursed business will lose first their hair, she said, then their eyes, their noses, and ears, and in the end the flesh will fall from their bones piece by piece.

Meanwhile the workmen, always in haste, scrambled day and night among the mesh of scaffolding, scurrying everywhere like beetles, with pails, whetstones, and stone slabs in their hands. It seemed that they were cladding the sides, because, in contrast to the stones of the piers and arches, this was soft limestone, which was easy to smooth, and was therefore called female stone. It was said that in some buildings in which it had been used long ago, it oozed a white juice, resembling milk, as if it were a woman's breast.

45

AT DAWN on the morning of the first Sunday of the month of St Dimiter, the bridge over the Ujana e Keqe, which had in these two years brought us more troubles than the river itself had brought stones and tree-stumps, stood complete.

Everyone knew that it was almost finished, but its appearance on that morning was quite fantastic. This was because the day before much of it had still been half hidden behind the confusion of planks, and they had only begun removing the scaffolding, as if peeling the husk from a corn cob, just before dusk. They had perhaps planned it this way, so that at the dawn of day it would stand clear, as if emerging from the womb of the gorge.

The hammers had echoed all night, dislodging the wooden wedges that fell crashing down. In their sleep, people thought they heard thunderclaps, turned heavily in their beds, and cursed or were afraid. There were many who thought that the labourers, repenting or following an order from who knows where, were demolishing what they had built.

In the morning, they were right not to believe their eyes. Under the surly light of day, between the turbid waters and the gloomy sky, it soared powerfully up from the bank, abrupt, dazzling, harsh as a scream, and hung in suspense over the watery gulf as if about to launch itself in flight. But as soon as it reached midway over the river, it dropped in its trajectory, like a dream of flying, and gently it bent its back until its span touched the opposite bank and froze there. It was lovely as a vision. The veins of the stone seemed both to absorb and emit light, like the pores of a living body. Caught between the enmity of water and earth, it now seemed as if striving to strike some accord between the separate elements of its surroundings. The frothing wave crests seemed to soften towards it, as did the wild pomegranate bushes on the opposite hill, and two small clouds on the horizon.

They all strove to make room for it in their midst. Here is its shape: Three arches ⋂⋂⋂ and the cross † that marked the place of sacrifice.

People stood in awe on both sides of the Ujana and gaped at it open-mouthed, as if it were a thing at once wicked and beautiful. Nevertheless nobody cursed it. Not even old Ajkuna, who came at midday, could curse it. The sight of it has turned me to stone, she seemed to say as she departed. In their total absorption in the spectacle, nobody paid the least attention to the throng of labourers preparing to leave. It was incredible that this mass of men and equipment, this pig run, this gang of vagrants that had tried the patience of wood and stone, this filth, this pack of stammerers, liars, boozers, hunchbacks, baldheads, and murderers, could have given birth to this miracle in stone.

Off to one side, as if they themselves felt that they had suddenly become alien to their own creation, they gathered their paraphernalia, tools, mortar buckets, hammers, ropes, and criminals' knives. They heaved them helter-skelter onto carts and mules, and, as I watched them scurrying about the bridge for the last time, I felt impatient, wanting them to leave the bridge. I wanted to be rid of them as soon as possible, and never hear of them again.

46

THE LAST contingent of workmen left three days later. They loaded on carts the heavy tools, great mortar barrels, and all kinds of scrap iron and wheels that creaked endlessly. They lifted the architect's sick assistant onto a covered cart, hiding him from people's view, because they said that his appearance was not for human eyes.

The deserted sandbank resembled a ruin, an eyesore with half-destroyed sheds stripped of everything of value, fragments of plank thrown any old where, traces of dried mortar, piles of shattered stones, broken tools carelessly discarded, ditches and lime-pits half-filled with water. The right bank of the Ujana looked disfigured for ever.

Before he boarded his cart, the foreman, who seemed to notice that I was watching their departure, left his people and came up to me, apparently to bid me farewell. He said nothing but merely drew a piece of card from his jacket. Scribbling some figures on it with a bit of lead, he began, I have no idea why, to explain to me the compensating forces that held the bridge upright. I stared at him because I had not the slightest knowledge of such things, while he went on in his disjointed way in the belief that he was explaining to me what the forces and counterforces were.

Late that afternoon, the final cart left and a frightening silence descended. I still had in my hand the draughtsman's card, covered with lines and figures, which perhaps did show the forces that kept the bridge upright and those trying to bring it down. The setting sun gleamed obliquely on the arches, which the waters at last brokenly reflected, and at that moment the bridge resembled a meaningless dream, dreamed by the river and both riverbanks together. So alien, dropped by the riverbanks into time, it looked totally solitary as it gripped in its stone limbs its only prey, Murrash Zenebisha, the man who died to allay the enmity of land and water.

47

WHAT HAD happened? They had gone and an unendurable silence reigned everywhere. A horrible calm. Almost as if plague had struck.

No one crossed the bridge. Not even Gjelosh the idiot. Chill winds blew upon it, passing in and out of its arches. And then the winds dropped and the bridge hung in air, alien and superfluous. Human travellers, who should have headed for it, avoided the place, turning aside, turning back, looking for the ford, calling softly to the ferryman; they were ready to swim across the river or freeze in its rapids and drown rather than set foot on the bridge. Nobody wanted to walk over the dead man.

And so the first week passed and the second began. The great mass of stone waited expectantly. The empty arches had about them a hungry look. The humped back of the bridge waited for someone to set foot on it, no matter whose – vagrants, women, barbarian hordes, wedding processions, imperial armies trampling across it, two, four, twenty-four, one hundred hours at a stretch.

But nobody set foot on it. Sometimes it made you want to cry out: Had so much sweat, so much effort, and even . . . blood been expended for this bridge, all to no purpose?

Rain fell the second week. For days on end, the bridge stood drenched and miserable.

Then the rain stopped and again the weather was chill and grey. The third week began. A moaning wind crawled over the waste land. It was the end of Tuesday afternoon when they saw that a wolf had padded softly over the bridge, as in a fairy tale. People could not credit their own eyes (and there were those who were ready to believe that a herald had crossed, waving the standard of the Skuraj family, the only one that has a wolf in its centre). The beast meanwhile vanished quickly into the distance, where the wind seemed to have stood still, and howled.

The days that followed were silent and empty. It was ashen weather everywhere, as if before the end of the world. One afternoon, old Ajkuna came up to the bridge. People thought that finally she would curse it, and they gathered to watch. She halted at the entrance to the bridge, below the right-hand approach arch, and laid her hand and then her ear to the masonry. She stood there a long while, then lifted her head from the palm of her hand, and said:

"It is trembling."

I remembered the man who had fallen in a epileptic fit. He had indeed passed on his convulsions to the bridge.

Many believed that the bridge would collapse of its own accord. Occasionally I brought out the card on which the designer had scribbled those mysterious figures, and I would study them abstractedly, as if trying to decipher in them the bridge's fear.

I would have wished that the designer could have seen this desolation.

But the bridge's quaking, which seemed ready to last

for centuries, came to an end suddenly one Sunday. The highway, the surrounding plain, and the sandbank echoed to an ear-shattering racket. People ran in terror to see what was happening. On the ancient highway, in a long black column, like a crawling iron reptile, a convoy of carts was travelling. The carts approached the bridge. We all stood frozen on the bank, expecting to witness some catastrophe. The first cart quickened its pace and began to mount the incline. You could hear the iron wheels changing their tone as they struck the stone paving. Then the cart mounted the right-hand approach arch, and then on, on, over the hump of the first arch, over . . . the dead man. Then came the second and third carts, and then the others, all laden with blackened barrels. They squeaked frighteningly, especially when they passed over the immured victim, and it looked each time as if the arch would split, but nothing happened.

The tail of the convoy was still on the bridge when people realized what kind of caravan it was, what it carried, and where it was going. Its sole cargo was pitch, for the Orikum military base near Vlora.

We watched its progress for a long time, looking alternately at the tail of the convoy and the bridge, which had suffered no harm at all.

Immediately after the crossing of this inauspicious tar train, as a guest at the Inn of the Two Roberts called it, news came that the death of Komneni had at last been announced at Vlora, and the troops of Balsha II had taken over the entire principality, including half of Orikum. Our count, accompanied by his entourage, departed to attend the old prince's burial. He must have been still on the road when, like thunder after a lightning flash, more news came, worse than the first, to tell us that the Byzantine garrison had finally evacuated the naval base and the Turkish garrison had taken over.

This meant that we were on the brink of war.

48

THE COUNT returned from Komneni's funeral even more withdrawn than when he had left. Almost all the lords of Arberia had gone to the ceremony, but apparently not even the sight of the old prince's coffin, around which they were all gathered perhaps for the last time, could give them the wisdom finally to reach an understanding among themselves.

Silence again reigned through all the days that followed. Still nobody else had crossed the bridge. One day only some frightened sheep somehow found themselves on it, tried to turn back, but were unable to do so. The sheep ran across the bridge while the terrified shepherd brandished his crook on the bank, calling for the ferryman to carry him across.

This was the only event of these days. A few blades of grass sprouted among the piles of stone and sand left beside the bridge. They were the first sign that nature was slowly, very slowly, but insistently preparing to erase from the face of the earth every trace that witnessed to the presence of workmen on the bank of the Ujana e Keqe.

The days were numb with cold, with a few motionless clouds in the distant sky, and silent, silent. No news came from anywhere. They said that in a very distant country they were building a great wall. The heart of Europe was once again ravaged by plague.

On the eleventh of the month of Michaelmas I was entrusted with a mission as far as the borders of our territories, where the domain of the neighbouring Turkish pasha begins. After completing my task, I would sit for hours on end, contemplating the point where the Turkish Empire began. I could not believe it was there in front of me. I repeated to myself over and over again, like someone wandering in his mind, that what they call the lands of Islam began a few paces in front of me. Asia began two paces in front of me. It was indeed enough to turn your wits. What had once been more distant than the lands of fairy-tales was now in front of our very noses. And still I could not believe it. Nor could anybody believe that these people had really come so close. There they were, yet evidence, times, dates, and the units of measurement of time and space dissolved as if in a mist. Sometimes I wanted to call out: Where are they? Below, the land was the same, and the same winter sky spanned the earth. And yet just here began, or rather ended, their enormous state, which spread from the deserts of China.

I had seen nobody on the other side during the days of my tour of duty, neither guards nor inhabitants. There was only land left waste, more like a stony desert, and scrub everywhere. Only on the last night (oh, if only I had not stayed that night), on that final night I heard their music. I still do not know where that singing, that music came from, who was singing, or why. I wonder whether they were wandering dervishes caught on the border as night fell, or civil servants sent from the capital to set border stones, or a group of itinerant musicians. In the end, I did not worry much about it. But when I heard their singing accompanied by entirely unfamiliar instruments, I felt seized by a sensation I had never known before. It was a drab sense of anxiety, without the slightest hint of hope. What was this stupor, this hashish dissolved in the air in the form of song? Its tones slithered drowsily, everything seemed sticky and shapeless. So this was their music, I thought, their inmost voice. It crept towards us like soporific mist. At its tones, feet skipping in a dance would falter as if seized by terror.

I returned heartsick from my journey.

Nothing noteworthy happened until the middle of the month, apart from the appearance of the body of a drowned man floating one day on the surface of the waters. It collided with the pier where the body was immured (the water level had now risen this far), twirled round, and struck the pier once again with its elbow, as if to say to the dead man, "How are you, brother." Then it floated away.

Those who had seen the drowned man and tried to tell other people were met with stares of incredulity. But that happened last year, people said. We saw it together. Don't you remember? And both sides would sit in bewilderment. By the bridge piers, time, swirling like water, seemed to have stood still.

49

O NE MORNING I was woken before dawn to be told
that people were crossing the bridge.

"Who?" I asked sleepily.

"The Baltaj family, all the men of the house together,
with their black ox."

I went up to the narrow window-slit that overlooked the
bridge. I knew that one day human beings would set foot
on it, but I did not think it would happen so soon. By next
spring at the earliest, I thought. Besides, I was also sure that
the first to dare would be some lone individual, not the
Baltajs with their flock of children.

"Where are they going?" I wonder. "What has got into
them?" I asked nobody in particular.

"No doubt some problem," called a voice from below.

Problem, I thought. What else could those black sheepskins contain?

The first sheepskin, the tallest of them, which was
leading the ox, emerged at the opposite bank, without
suffering any harm. After him came the shorter ones, and
finally the children.

"They've crossed," somebody said.

They expected me to say something, perhaps a curse or,
on the contrary, a blessing on the travellers. Perhaps they
had for a long time felt a secret wish to cross the bridge.

I had experienced something of this sort myself, and whenever I felt its pull I would walk to and fro for a long while, tiring my legs, as if this desire were simply in my legs alone, and I were punishing them for it.

So the Baltajs had crossed . . . but only their menfolk. I remembered that in the villages crossing the rainbow was considered so impossible that people thought that any girl who went over could be turned into a boy . . . And suddenly it flashed into my mind that nothing other than a rainbow must have been the first sketch for a bridge, and the sky had for a long time been planting this primordial form in people's minds . . .

I felt afraid of all this hostility towards the bridge. However, I calmed myself at once. The divine model had been pure. But here, although the bridge pretended to embody this idea, it had death at its foundations.

The Baltajs, who had sold their black ox because of some pressing need, returned bitter and disconsolate, crossing the bridge again, but without their animal. Everybody talked about their crossing, but there was neither anger nor reproach in their words. There was only something like a sigh.

In the meantime Uk the ferryman had fallen ill. He had caught cold, which was not in itself something unexpected. But when it became known, everyone seemed to be astonished. Night and day on that dilapidated raft, his feet in the water, forty and more years on end. How had he gone all that time without catching his death?

Indeed he died soon and was buried on the same day. It was a cloudy afternoon. The Ujana e Keqe was full of waves, and the blackened raft, moored to its jetty by chains, bucked on the waters like a nervous horse that had sensed the death of its master.

"Ferries and Rafts" did not replace the ferryman. It did not even remember the abandoned raft. The post that supported the sign with its name and the tolls was now very unsteady, and one day someone took it away.

As if the ferryman's death were some long-awaited signal, people one after another began to use the bridge. After the Baltajs, the Kryekuqe family crossed the bridge, and after them the landlord of the Inn of the Two Roberts, together with his brother-in-law, both pickled. On the same day, some foreign pilgrims crossed and at midday on the eighteenth of the month large numbers of the Stres clan passed over, a pregnant woman among them.

None of the Zenebishas crossed. There were also many old men and women, led by old Ajkuna, who not only vowed never to commit the sin of setting foot on that devil's backbone, but had left instructions in their wills that even after their deaths they would prefer their coffins to be hurled into the water rather than carried over the bridge to the graveyard on the opposite bank.

Meanwhile, the abandoned raft tied by its chain to the old jetty rotted and crumbled in an extraordinarily short time. Such a thing was indeed surprising, especially when you think that the ferryman had made virtually no repairs for decades. People had only to give up using it for a very short while before it disintegrated.

50

ON THE morning of the third of the month of St Ndreu,
early in the morning, Dan Mteshi crossed the bridge,
together with his sons and a goat. After him, the men of the
Gjorg clan crossed on their way to the law court. Then
Gjelosh the idiot crossed (or rather advanced to the middle
and turned back). Later, all noise and laughter, almost the
entire Vulkathanaj clan crossed, mounted on mules, travelling
to a wedding in Buzëzesta. Immediately afterwards, Duda's
daughters crossed, as did Gjelosh the idiot, once again making
a zigzag path. At midday, two groups of strangers crossed
immediately after each other, and then a drunkard from the
Inn of the Two Roberts; then Gjelosh the idiot braced himself
to set off again, but did not do so. Towards dusk, on his bay
mount, the knight Stanish Stresi crossed as fast as you could
blink, though nobody could say why, and after him a foreign
herald. When night fell, crossings became very rare, and travellers were anyway no longer recognizable in the darkness.
As their silhouettes appeared on the bridge, you could gather
a little from their gait, such as whether they were Arberians
or foreigners, but there was no way that you could tell why
they were travelling, whether for pleasure, penance, or murder.

51

Not a living soul crossed the bridge for one hundred hours in a row. Rain fell. The horizon was dissolved in mist. They said that plague was ravaging central Europe.

What was this interruption? For a time it seemed that people, having committed such a sin (and there were those who went to confession immediately after crossing the bridge), had made an agreement to abandon the bridge for good. However, on Sunday night the traffic resumed as unexpectedly as it had ceased.

When I was at leisure, I enjoyed choosing a sheltered spot and observing the bridge. The bridge was like an open book. As I watched the comings and goings, it seemed to me that I could grasp its essence. It sometimes seemed to me that human confidence, fear, suspicion, and madness were nowhere more clearly manifest than on its back. Some people stole over, as if afraid of damaging it, while others went stamping across it.

There were those who continued to cross at night, bandit-style, as if scared of somebody, or perhaps of the bridge itself, since they had spoken so ill of it.

After the bishop of Ardenica, who was travelling to defrock a priest at the Monastery of the Three Crosses, another covered wagon crossed, which, it was later suspected, probably contained an abducted woman. Then came oil traders.

Gjelosh the idiot followed the traders, shouting, because it was well known that he could not endure the seepages from their skin bottles. With a rag in his hand, he would stagger almost on his knees, wiping away the traces of oil, and with the same rag wiping the bridge parapets, as if to clean them of dust.

Late in the afternoon, there came, from who knows where, Shtjefen Keqi and Mark Kasneci, or Mark Haberi as he had recently begun to call himself. They had set off a week ago with a great deal of fuss "to look death in the eye", but, it seemed, were coming back as always with their tails between their legs.

Two months previously, Mark Kasneci had caused us a great deal of confusion with his new surname. After a trip to the fiefdom of the Turkish pasha, he came back and announced that he was no longer called Mark Kasneci but Mark Haberi, which has the same meaning of "herald" in Turkish. He was the first person to change his surname, and people went in some perplexity to see him. He was the same Mark Kasneci as he had always been, the same in flesh and bone, but now with a different name. I summoned him to the parish house and said, "Mark, they say that along with your surname you have also changed your religion." But he swore to me that that was not true. When I told him that a surname was not a cap you could change whenever you liked, he begged me with tears in his eyes to forgive him and to let him come to church, because, although he felt he was a sinner, he liked the surname so much and would not be parted from it . . .

That is what people are like. It sometimes occurred to me that if the bridge had a mind, it would be more disgusted than amused by us and would take to its heels like a frightened beast. A rainbow, the bridge's model and perhaps its inspiration, is something that, thank God, nobody yet knows how to build, and still less to chain in fetters. But is it not also something frightening, fragile, and incomprehensible to people?

52

A T THE end of the week, the two representatives of
the bridge owners, mounted on mules, turned up
again after being absent for so long. People gaped at them
open-mouthed when they arrived, as if they were seeing
shades. People's eyes followed them, as if asking: Still on
this earth?

They themselves did not spare a glance for the bridge,
not even for the dead man in the first arch, but they applied
themselves immediately to the task for which they had
come. They dug two holes, one at each end of the bridge,
fixed iron poles in them, and secured metal signs on the
poles, like those once used by "Ferries and Rafts". It was
understood at once that these were tables of bridge tolls.
Everything was set out in detail, the toll for individuals,
reduced rates for whole families and clans, the toll for the
crossing of each head of livestock, reductions for herds,
the toll for individual carts, reductions for caravans, and
so forth.

People looked at the sign as if to say, "We turned our
noses up before at crossing for free, and now we have
to pay!"

The two employees of the road and bridge company did
not leave after erecting the signs, but took over the ferryman's small abandoned shed, which, it seems, the company

had bought some time before. They began to do duty at the bridge in turns.

And the odd thing was that people began to cross the bridge in greater numbers after the toll was imposed.

53

A VENETIAN monk on his way to Byzantium brought
more bad news from the Vlora base. A Turkish imperial decree had just been issued, removing the base's old
name of Orikum, and renaming it Pasha-Liman. This was
a terrifying and in any event an extraordinary name, since
in Turkish it meant "port of ports", "chief port", or "pasha
of ports". It was not hard to imagine what a military base
with such a name would be used for. This was a great
harbour opened by the Ottomans on Europe's very flank.

As the monk told me, Albanian and Turkish soldiers
provoked each other daily at the boundary dividing the
Vlora base. Dim-witted as he was, Balsha II could easily fall
into a trap.

After the monk left, I went for a long walk on the banks
of the Ujana e Keqe, and my thoughts were as murky as its
waters. Time and again, that music of death I had heard
weeks ago on the border came to my mind. Yes, they were
trying to shackle our feet with that enervating music. And
after halting our dances they would bind our hands and
then our souls.

The hunger of the great Ottoman state could be felt in
the wind. We were already used to the savage hunger of the
Slavs. Naked and with bared teeth like a wolf's, this hunger
always seemed more dangerous than anything else. But, in

contrast, the Ottoman pressure involved a kind of seduction. It struck me as no accident that they had chosen the moon as their symbol. Under its light, the world could be caressed and lulled to sleep more easily.

As I walked along the riverbank, this caress terrified me more than anything else. Dusk was falling. The bridge looked desolate and cold. And suddenly, in its slightly hunched length, in its arches, buttresses, and in its solitude, there was air of expectancy. What are you waiting for, stone one, I said to myself. Distant phantoms? Or an imperial army and the sound of nameless feet, marching ten, twenty, a hundred hours without rest? A curse upon you!

54

NEWS FOLLOWED hard on news, as regular and grim as clouds in the stormy season. The Turks had launched a major diplomatic offensive. More than half the Balkan peninsula was now under the Ottoman crescent. Indeed three of the eleven lords of Arberia had also accepted vassalage. Throughout the Balkans, Turkish armies were on large-scale manoeuvres in order to strike fear into those princes and dukes who had yet to swear fealty. The famous "Arbanon Line" was crumbling, the seven fortresses from Shkodra to Lezha, which defended Byzantium from the Slavs. Byzantium itself seemed under threat. The Balkan nobles – Albanians, Croats, Greeks, Serbs, Romanians, Macedonians, and Slovenes – sent their couriers to Venice one day, to Turkey the next, and sometimes to both at once, to choose the lesser of the two dangers. It was said that while the messengers left by one door, at another entered soothsayers – drawers of straws and especially readers of shoulder-blades, as people had recently called those who predict the approach or retreat of war by the colour of a ram's shoulder-blade. It was said that immediately after one dinner, at which the reader of the shoulder-blade was horrified by the reddish tinge of the bone, the Count of the Skurajs sent messengers to the sultan. The Muzakas were also wavering. The stand of the Dukagjins was unknown.

They had withdrawn into the depths of the mountains, as they usually did at such times, and were brooding behind the mists. There is always time to die, their forebear is supposed to have said. However, the phrase has been considered ambiguous because it is not clear which is considered death, the acceptance of war or of vassalage. The Dukagjins had never been sycophants, but nevertheless at such times anything could happen.

Increasingly often, I remembered their emblems with all their lions' manes, fangs, claws, and cockspurs, as if to determine the stand they would take . . . Just as often, I remembered the laughter of the two countesses on the bank of the Ujana e Keqe, when they flirted with the name of "Abdullahth", and then their gossip about their sister-in-law Katrina, or "the queen" as they sarcastically called her, because her husband Karl Topia was a pretender to the long-vacant throne of Arberia. I remembered all these things and became as frightened of these dainty women as of the Turkish yataghan. I was frightened of the gifts and silks with which the Ottomans were so generous, and that the ladies coveted so much.

Some time ago, when the Count of Kashnjet and the Duke of Tepelena had been the first to accept vassalage, they had mocked those who had predicted disaster. You said that the Turks would destroy us and strip us and disgrace us, they said. But we are still masters of our lands. Our castles are still where they were; our coats of arms, our honour, and our possessions are untouched. If you don't believe us, come and see with your own eyes.

That is how they, and their ladies especially, wrote to other nobles. In fact, it was true in a way. The Turk did not touch them. Nothing had changed, except for one

151

apparently insignificant detail . . . This was the matter of the date at the head of their letters. Instead of the year 1378, they had written "*hijrah* 757", according to the Islamic calendar, which was one of the Ottomans' few demands.

How unlucky they were. They had turned the clock back six hundred years, and they laughed and joked. How could they!

55

NEVER BEFORE had so many travellers stayed at the Inn of the Two Roberts. They also brought us news, most of it, alas, bleak.

The Muzakas had sent back the Ottomans' third deputation. The two barons Gropa and Matranga, on the contrary, had declared their vassalage. So had two Serbian kings in the frontier regions and another Croatian prince. It was not yet known what Nikollë Zaharia and his vassals had decided, nor the Kastriotis. There were whispers about an alliance between the two most powerful nobles, the great Count Karl Topia and Balsha II, but this could just as well be wishful thinking as the truth. The question of the crown, to which Topia was a pretender, was an almost insuperable obstacle to such a pact. Others said that Topia had sent his own messengers to forge an alliance with the King of Hungary. As for old Balsha, he had withdrawn to the mountains like the Dukagjins, and besides, he was too old to lead a campaign. Nevertheless, singly and in wretched isolation, some in twos or occasionally in threes, the majority of the Albanian nobles were preparing for war. Count Stres, our liege lord, also called on all his vassals and knights to stand by.

We were on the brink of war, and only the blind could fail to see it. Since the Ottoman state became our neighbour, I do not look at the moon as before, especially when it is a crescent. No empire has so far chosen a more masterful symbol for its flag. When Byzantium chose the eagle, this was indeed superior to the Roman wolf, but now the new empire has chosen an emblem that rises far higher in the skies than any bird. It has no need to be drawn like our cross, or to be cut in cloth and hoisted above castle turrets. It climbs into the sky itself, visible to the whole of mankind, with nothing to mask the view of it. Its meaning is more than clear: the Ottomans will settle accounts not with one state or two states, but with the whole world. Your flesh creeps when you see it, cold, sometimes honey-coloured and occasionally the colour of blood. Sometimes I think that it is already casting a spell on us from above. There is a danger that one day, like sleepwalkers, we will rise up to walk towards our ruin.

Last night as I prayed, I unconsciously replaced the words of the holy book, "Let there be light," with "Let there be Arberia!" almost as if Arberia had in the meantime been undone . . .

I myself was terrified by this inner voice. Later, when I tried to discover whence it came, I recalled all kind of discussions and predictions now being made about the future of this country. Arberia will find itself several times on the verge of the abyss. Like a tumbling stone, it will draw sparks and blood. The saying is that it will be made and unmade many times before it stands fixed for all time on the face of the earth. So, let there be Arberia!

56

DESPITE THE great frost, there are Turkish troop movements on the border. The drums are inaudible, but their banners can be discerned from a distance.

One morning, sentries of the principality appeared at both ends of the bridge. Our liege lord's estrangement from the neighbouring pasha had deepened.

The armed guards remained at the bridge day and night, next to the signs with the tolls. We thought this must be a temporary measure, but after three days the guards were not withdrawn, but reinforced.

Dark news was coming at us from all sides. It seems that old Balsha had gone completely blind, night coming to his eyes before invading his soul. As the saying goes, "May I not see what tomorrow holds in store!"

57

MEANWHILE, AS if not caring about what was happening throughout the Balkans, travellers whose road brought them this way, or rich men journeying to see the world, paused increasingly often at the bridge. This had become so common recently that the landlord of the Inn of the Two Roberts had placed a kind of notice at both his gates, written in four languages: "For those guests desiring to see the famous Three-Arched Bridge, with the man immured within, the inn provides outward and return journeys at the following rates . . ." (There followed the tariff in various currencies.)

A large cart drawn by four horses and equipped with elevated seats carried the guests to and from the bridge two or three times a day and sometimes more often. Loud-mouthed and boorish, as idle travellers usually tend to be, they swarmed round and under the bridge, noticing everything with curiosity, touching the piers, crouching under the approach arches, and lingering by the first arch where the man was walled up. Their polyglot, monotonous, and interminable chatter took over the site. I went among them several times to eavesdrop on this jabbering, which was always the same and somehow different from the previous day's. The flow of time seemed to have stood still. They talked about the legend and the bridge, asked questions and sought explanations from each other, confused the old legend with the death of Murrash Zenebisha, and tried to sort matters out, but only confused them further, until the cart from the inn would arrive, bringing a fresh contingent of travellers and taking away the previous one. Then everything would start again from the beginning. "So this whole bridge was built by three brothers?" "No, no, that's what the old legend says. This was built by a rich man who also surfaces roads and sells tar. He has his own bank in Durrës." "But how was this man sacrificed here, if it's all an old legend?" "I think there is no room for misunderstanding, sir. He sacrificed himself, to appease the spirits of the water, and in exchange for a huge sum in compensation paid to his family." "Ah, so it was a question of water spirits; but you told me it had no connection with the legend." "I'm not saying it has no connection, but . . . the main thing was business of the compensation."

And then they would begin talking about the compensation, whistling in amazement at the enormous sum, calculating the percentages the members of his family would earn from the bridge's profits, and converting the sums into the currencies of their own principalities, and then into Venetian ducats. And so, without anyone noticing, the conversation would leave the bridge behind and concentrate on the latest news from the Exchange Bank in Durrës, particularly on the fluctuating values of various currencies and the fall in the value of gold sovereigns following the recent upheavals on the peninsula. And this would continue until some traveller, coming late to the crowd, would ask: "They seemed to tell us that it was a woman who was walled up, but this is a man. They even told us that we would see the place where the milk from the poor woman's breast dripped." "Oh," two or three voices would reply simultaneously, "are you still thinking of the old legend?"

And the whole discussion would start up again from the beginning.

58

IT WAS Mark Haberi who was the first to bring the news of the Turks' "commination" against Europe from across the border. Pleased that the event seemed so important to me, he looked at me with eyes that reminded me of my displeasure at his change of surname, almost as if, without that Turkish surname, he would not be able to bring news, in other words *habere*, from over there.

Indeed, his explanation of what had happened was so involved that, while he talked, he became drenched with sweat, like a man who fears to be taken for a liar. Speak clearly, I said to him two or three times, because I cannot understand what you are trying to say. But he continued to prevaricate. I can't say it, he repeated. These are new, frightening things, that cannot be put into words.

He asked my permission to explain by gestures, making movements that struck me as demented. I told him that the gesture he was making is among us called a "fig", and indicates at the same time contempt, indifference, and a curse. He cried, "Precisely, father. There they call it a 'commination' and it has the force of law."

I did not conceal my amazement at the connection between this hand movement, which people and especially women make in contempt of each other, somewhat in the sense of "may my ill-luck be on your head," with the new

Ottoman state policy towards Europe, of which Mark Haberi sought to persuade me.

He stalked off and went to collect additional tidings, which he indeed brought me a few days later, still from the other side. They left me open-mouthed. From his words and the testimony of others that I heard in those days, I reconstructed the entire event, like a black temple.

The Commination Against Europe had taken place in the last days of the month of Michaelmas, precisely on the Turkish-Albanian border, and had been performed according to all the ancient rubrics in the archives of the Ottoman state. Their rules of war demanded that, before any battle started, the place about to be attacked, whether a castle, a wall, or simply an encampment, had to be cursed by the army's curse-maker.

It was said that the old archives described precisely, even with the help of a sketch, the gesture of the curse. The palms of the hand were opened and moved forward, as if to launch the portentous curse on its flight. This gesture was repeated three times and then the back was turned on the direction in which the curse was headed.

Their chronicles told of the cursing of castles and the domains of rebellious pashas, and even whole states, before an attack began; but there was no case of an entire continent being cursed. It was perhaps for this reason that even the most important curse-maker in the state, Sukrullah, who had arrived on the empire's extreme border the previous night, looked slightly shaken, as those who saw him reported.

The sky was overcast and damp and the whole plain around the small temporary minaret erected specially for the purpose was swathed in mist.

The curse-maker climbed the little minaret and stared for a while in our direction, towards where, in their eyes, the accursed continent of Europe began. The weather was indeed extremely bad, and almost nothing could be seen in the fog. The small group of high dignitaries who had accompanied Sukrullah from the capital to the border stood mute. Down below, at the foot of the minaret, the imperial chronicler had opened a thick tome to record the event.

Sukrullah raised his arms in front of him, so that they emerged from the wide sleeves of his semi-clerical gown. Everybody saw that the palms of his hands were exceptionally broad. However, nobody was surprised at this, because he was not the state's foremost curse-maker for nothing.

He studied his hands for a while, and, turning his eyes towards the murky distance, he raised his palms in front of his face to the level of his brow. His palms paled as the blood drained from them. He held them there for a time until they were as white as the palms of a corpse, and then thrust them violently forward, as if the evil were in the form of a bubble he was dispatching into the distance.

He did this three times in a row. The commination was complete.

In silence he climbed down from the minaret, followed immediately by his escorts. Together with the other officials, they accompanied him to his carriage, whose doors were embellished with the emblem of the Great Imperial Commination. He climbed into the carriage together with his assistants and guards, and, as the vehicle departed through the winter cold in the direction from which it had come, the curse travelled in the opposite direction, towards us, towards the lands of Europe. It went (or rather came) through the fog, like some bird of ill omen, like a herald, or a sick dream.

So, God on high, there it is! What sort of country is this with which fate has embroiled us? What signs it sends through the air to us. And what else will it send after them?

59

THE MONTH of St Ndreu began and ended in fog. Sometimes the fog seemed to freeze stock still. Everything half dissolved in it: the riverbanks, the nearby hamlets, the bleak sandbank, the bridge. On such days of mist, the victim immured in the lap of the bridge seemed both more remote and closer, as if he would shortly resolve his ambiguous position, and would step out towards us, a living man towards the living, or would retreat, a dead man towards the dead.

But he remained in between, neither in this world nor the next, and a constant burden to us all. Nobody knew what had happened to his flesh inside, but his whitewashed mask was still the same. His open, vacant eyes, his cheeks, lips, and chin were the same as before. Sometimes a drop of moisture would appear on his features, as if on the surface of a wall, and would leave a mark when it dried.

There were people who stayed for a long time, trying to decipher these signs. There were noisy crowds, also, who chattered under his very nose, shook their fingers in front of his eyes, and even made slighting remarks about him. Anybody else, suspended in his position, would not dream of anything but gathering his own bones in some grave. It was believed that lightning frightened him, while the ravens no longer came swooping over him.

His family's visits became increasingly rare. They now no longer came in two hostile groups, but in four: his wife and baby, his parents, and his two brothers separately. Their quarrel over sharing the compensation had deepened during the autumn, and the law suit they had initiated over its division would be, it seemed, hopelessly protracted.

Each party came and stayed a while by the whitewash mask, as if before a court, with their own explanations and worries. The man's open eyes stared at them all impartially, while the visitors no doubt imagined that next time they would reach a better understanding with the whitewash.

Next time . . . There were indeed days on which it seemed that he would tear himself free of his enveloping plaster to come and talk things out with them. It would be his turn to judge perhaps not only his kith and kin but the entire human race.

I have seen statues age, but I have the feeling that this bas-relief, perhaps the only one in the world with the dead man's flesh, bones, and maybe soul inside it, will have a different life expectancy. Either it will burst into pieces prematurely, or it will outlive all others. The seasons will deposit their dust on it, the wind will slowly, very slowly erode it, as it erodes all the world, and he, Murrash Zenebisha, who has now donned his protective mask, and for whom the years have stopped, will eventually find old age. But old age will not come by years and seasons, in the normal way of human age, but by centuries. Sometimes I say to myself: Poor you, Murrash Zenebisha. What horrors you will see. For the future seems to me pregnant only with terrible disasters. But sometimes I think to myself: You are fortunate in what you will see, because, whatever will happen, I am sure that like every storm, this too will pass, just as every night finds a dawn.

60

THE BLOODSHED occurred one day before Christmas, at four in the afternoon. Everything took place in a very short time, the bat of an eyelid, but it was an event of the kind that is able to divide time in two. Since that day in the month of St Ndreu, people do not talk about time in general, they talk about time before and time after.

Until shortly before that fatal moment, four o'clock (on that cloudy day, it seemed to have been four o'clock since morning), there was no ominous sign anywhere. Everything looked bare, when suddenly, God knows how, the chill fog spawned seven horsemen. They were approaching at speed with a curious kind of gallop, not in a straight line, but describing wide arcs, as if an invisible gale were driving their horses first in one direction and then in another. When they drew near enough to distinguish their helmets and breastplates, they were seen to be Turkish horsemen.

When our sentries on the right bank saw that the horsemen were making for the bridge, they took up their stations and crossed their spears. The horsemen continued their onrush towards the bridge in their unusual gallop, describing arcs. Our sentries commanded them to halt. They were required to stop, even if they had crossed the border with permission, and all the more so if they had come without permission, which had often happened recently. But the horsemen did not obey.

To those who witnessed the skirmish from the distance of the riverbank, it resembled a dumb show. Two of the Turkish horsemen were able to force their way through our guards and make for the middle of the bridge. A third was brought down from his mount, and a skirmish began around him. One of our guards ran after the horsemen who were racing ahead. Those left behind, Albanians and Turks, engaged spears. Another horseman succeeded in struggling free of the confusion, and went on the heels of our guard, who was pursuing the first two horsemen. Meanwhile, our sentries on the left side of the bridge were rushing to the help of their comrades. They met the first two Turkish horsemen at the centre of the bridge. An Albanian sentry pursuing the horsemen joined the fight, as did the third Turkish rider, who had pursued our guard.

Yet all this happened, as I said, in total silence, or seemed to, because the raging of the river smothered every sound. Only once (ah, my flesh creeps even now when I think of it), did a voice emerge from this wordless conflict. It was no human voice, it was a broken "kra", a horrible cry from some non-human throat. And then that play of shadows again, with somebody running from the middle of the bridge to the right bank, and returning to rescue someone who had fallen. There was a clash of spears, and at last the repulse of the horsemen, and their retreat into the fog out of which they had come, with one riderless horse neighing as it followed them.

That was all. The horizon swallowed the horsemen just as it had given them birth, and you could have thought they were only a mirage, but . . . there was evidence left at the bridge. Blood stained the bridge at its very mid-point.

The count himself soon came to the scene of the incident. He walked slowly across the bridge, while the guards, their breastplates scarred with spear scratches, told him what had happened. They paused by the pool of blood. It must have been the blood of the Turkish soldier, whose body the horsemen had succeeded in recovering. As the blood congealed, the stones of the gravel made its final gleam more visible.

"Turkish blood," our liege lord said in a hoarse, broken voice.

Nobody could tear his eyes away. We had seen their Asiatic costume. We had heard their music. Now we were seeing their blood . . . The only thing they had in common with us.

This day had been bound to come. It had long been travelling in the caravan of time. We had expected it, but perhaps not so suddenly, with those seven horsemen emerging from the mist and being swallowed by the mist again, followed by a riderless horse.

61

As the hours passed, the incident appeared ever more serious. Nightfall enlarged its significance in an extraordinary way. So did the days that followed. The silence that fell the following week, far from diminishing its importance, heightened it yet further. Those disjointed movements by our soldiers and the Turkish riders on the bridge, that seemed from a distance like the dance of madmen, were repeated in everybody's minds in slow motion, as if in delirium. They were like a first pass at war. It was obvious now that this had not been a chance incursion. From the base at Vlora to the mountains of the Dukagjins and the Kastriotis, the Turks had sparked off a series of provocations. You would have had to have less sense than Gjelosh to fail to realize that war had effectively begun.

On Sunday, as I walked late at night on the deserted sandbank (The idiot had wandered cackling over the bridge a short time before), I felt a greater depression than ever before. The moonlight fell evenly over the plain, freezing everything into a mask. Everything was wan; everything was dead, and I almost cried out: How can you become part of Asia, you, my lovely Arberia?

My eyes darkened and, just as I had seen that pale patch of blood under Murrash Zenebisha's neck, so it seemed to me that now, under that moonlight, I saw whole plains awash with blood, and mountain ranges burned to cinders. I saw Ottoman hordes flattening the world and creating in its place the land of Islam. I saw the fires and the ash and the scorched remains of men and their chronicles. And our music, and dances, and costume, and our majestic language, harried by that terrible "*-luk*", like a reptile's tail, seeking refuge in the mountains among the lightning and the beasts, which will turn it savage. And below the mountains, I saw the plains left without speech. And above all, I saw the long night coming in hours, for centuries . . .

Unconsciously, I had reached the bridge's first arch, where the immured man was. The moon illuminated him shockingly, and for a long time I stood there stunned, with my gaze fixed on his whitewashed eyes. I was cold, as if he were conveying to me the iciness of the next world. "Murrash Zenebisha," I said silently. (The thought that I was imitating Gjelosh the idiot, who once used to talk to the dead man like this, did not worry me in the least.) "Murrash Zenebisha," I repeated, "You died before me, but will live after me . . ." I could not muster the strength to tear my gaze away from the those quenched eyes, whose whiteness was becoming unendurable. Why had I come here? What did I want to tell him, and what did I expect of him? I should have run as fast as I could from the splashing of the moonlight and from that place of sacrifice, but my legs failed me. At any moment it seemed that the curtain of plaster would fall from the dead man's eyes, allowing his message to pass. I could almost decipher that message. We two are very close, monk, his eyes seemed to say. Do you not feel it?

I did indeed feel it precisely, and as I moved backwards without taking my eyes from him (for this seemed the only way to break away from him), I felt I should return to the parish house as soon as I could to complete my chronicle. I should return as soon as possible and finish it, because times are black; soon night may fall, it will be too late for everything, and we may pay with our lives for writing such testimonies. This was the immured man's message. And this chronicle, like the bridge itself, may demand a sacrifice, and that sacrifice can be none other than myself, I, the monk Gjon, sonne of Gjorg Ukcama, who hath finyshed this knowynge that ther is no thynge wryttene in owre tonge about the Brigge of the Ujana e Keqe and the euil whyche is upon us, and do it out of love of owre worlde.

Tirana, 1976–1978